SEPT. 16, 2017
For Tom
William P. Robertson

Misdeeds & Misadventures

Action Stories for Men

William P. Robertson

ISBN 978-1-4958-0932-3

Copyright © 2016 by William P. Robertson

All rights reserved, including the right of reproduction in any form, or by any mechanical or electronic means including photocopying or recording, or by any information storage or retrieval system, in whole or in part in any form, and in any case not without the written permission of the author and publisher.

This is a work of fiction. Names, characters, places, and incidents either are the product of the author's imagination or are used fictitiously. Any resemblance to actual events or locales or persons, living or dead, is entirely coincidental.

Published February 2016

INFINITY PUBLISHING
1094 New DeHaven Street, Suite 100
West Conshohocken, PA 19428-2713
Toll-free (877) BUY BOOK
Local Phone (610) 941-9999
Fax (610) 941-9959
Info@buybooksontheweb.com
www.buybooksontheweb.com

Contents

Acknowledgments 1
Author's Note 3
Union Gold 5
Guarding Lincoln 15
In Pairs 23
The Chasm 29
Each Summer Writes Its Own Story 35
Blackbirds 39
The Gangster 41
Finger and Thumb 45
Goosey 47
The Eight Point 53
The Speedboat 61
The River 71
The "Friendly" Coon 79
Kinzua Beach 87
The Panty Raid 95
The Infestation 105
The Fish Wardens 111
Fierce When Roused 123
The Attack 129
The Ace of Fire 135
Father's Gift 141
Ibin 147
Bibliography 149
Author's Profile 153

Acknowledgments

A special thanks to David Cox who designed the front and back covers. Contact him at dlcox4498@gmail.com. Thanks also to Tom Aaron for helping me research "Guarding Lincoln."

"Each Summer Writes Its Own Story" first appeared in the June 17, 2015, "'Round the Square" column in *The Bradford Era* newspaper, Bradford, Pennsylvania. "Finger and Thumb" was initially published in *Cokefish* magazine, Long Valley, New Jersey. "Ibin" appeared in *Premonitions*, Isle of Wight, England.

Colby Tupper's photo is courtesy of Joel Frampton Gilfert. It is included in the "Guarding Lincoln" story. Tupper was a corporal in the 150th Bucktail Regiment.

The photo used in "The Attack" is of John J. Finnessy, who was a captain in the 59th Infantry Regiment of the American Expeditionary Force in World War I. The pic is courtesy of Betty Finnessy. John's *History of the 59th* provided much of the information for this story.

Other photos are from the Robertson family album or were taken by William P. Robertson.

WILLIAM P. ROBERTSON

The front cover photo is of my grandfather, Paul Wellington Robertson. He looked like such a bad dude sitting on the motorcycle that I cast him as a gangster in the "Blackbirds" story. In real life he worked for the Erie Railroad as a conductor. His regular train route from Salamanca, New York, to Brockway, Pennsylvania, took him across the Kinzua Bridge every other day. He married my grandmother, Bernadine Johnson, and they had three children, Jane, Dick, and Paul W. Junior, who was my dad. The Robertson family lived on High Street in Bradford, Pennsylvania. Grandpa died on April 24, 1953, of lung cancer.

Author's Note

Ernest Hemingway was my biggest influence when I got serious about writing fiction. I first studied his work in graduate school at Mansfield University. The thing I liked most about him is that he was never pretentious. He was more interested in telling a riveting story than showing how smart he was. To accomplish this, he wrote in a journalistic style and used everyday words. He also drew heavily from his personal life, which made his material realistic. Equally impressive, he used irony to highlight his cynicism toward the violence of society. Nature was his escape, as it is mine.

My favorite work by Hemingway was his first collection of stories, *In Our Time*. I used this tome as a model for *Misdeeds and Misadventures*. Like Hemingway, a lot of my fiction is based on outdoor adventures I experienced. The rest of my stories are historical fiction war yarns or gangster tales derived from actual events. They get right to the point and often have surprise endings. Some are very short like the "Chapters" in Hemingway's book. I include plenty of vicious creatures, too, including coyotes and men drunk on lust.

Union Gold

When Lieutenant Castleton ripped open his orders and began to read, he broke into a nervous sweat. His mission was to deliver a shipment of gold bars from Wheeling, West Virginia, to the U.S. Mint in Philadelphia. The bars had been coated with black pitch paint to disguise them as lead and then placed under the false bottom of a wagon. For added subterfuge, the wagon was filled with hay. There were twenty-six fifty pound bars in all worth many thousands of dollars.

The lieutenant was assigned a squad of heavily-armed cavalry to escort him. Castleton chose for his guide a civilian he knew well. He was a woodsman named Connors who had grown up in the wilderness of Pennsylvania. Connors was as brawny as Castleton was lean and frail. He also had a shifty way about him that was noted by several troopers.

Jeff Marshall was the squad's sergeant. Although short in stature, he had won a chestful of medals fighting Indians in the Western Territories. He had a mean streak, too, that could only be satisfied by riding bulls or breaking wild horses. He sported a well-trimmed mustache under his nose, and his keen eyes missed nothing.

The Rebels had just won the Battle of Chancellorsville, and rumors of their invasion of Pennsylvania flew about like blackbirds flushed from a thicket. In his last-minute instructions Castleton was told to avoid enemy patrols at all costs, even if it meant riding deep into the mountains north of Pittsburgh.

After briskly saluting his commander, the lieutenant led his men from the fort. The wagon was pulled by a team of four mules, and the cavalry rode in front and behind it. Following the less traveled roads, they skirted Pittsburgh and then clattered toward the thriving lumber town of Butler.

The farther the lieutenant rode, the more his stomach churned. Sweat poured down his drawn face, and his brow burned with fever. Finally, he dismounted from his horse and climbed woozily into the wagon.

Sergeant Marshall bristled when Connors was put in charge of the expedition. "Cripes Alfriday," he protested. "Since when does a civilian lead the U.S. Calvary?"

"Since I outrank you," replied Castleton, issuing a sick cough. "That man knows every inch of the wilderness ahead."

The soldiers only stopped in Butler long enough to buy flour, bacon, and beans. The bluecoats drew suspicious stares, and the village wags immediately began guessing the purpose of their visit. Were they searching for boys to draft into the Union Army or to plan fortifications for the town? The Rebels were coming, after all, and why shouldn't ramparts be built there?

Sergeant Marshall, meanwhile, shooed away groups of curious children. "If I ain't been told the importance of this dang hay wagon, you scamps sure ain't gonna find out," he bellowed. "Now, git!" His gruff voice echoed halfway up the block and sent kids crying into their mothers' aprons.

The sharp tongues of offended dames chased after the Yankees when they headed down the street. Entering the Clarion Valley, they followed a road that was little more than an Indian path. The forest was thick, and clouds of mosquitoes harried them every mile of the way. Several times, the troopers had to dismount and kill a timber rattler or copperhead sunning itself on the trail. Connors kept the snakes and cooked quite a feast for dinner.

When the soldiers reached the village of Clarion the next morning, Lieutenant Castleton crawled from the wagon and disappeared into a dark tavern. There, he had a big plate of flapjacks and a sarsaparilla that brought the color back to his cheeks. After breakfast, he again climbed on his horse and led the expedition toward Ridgway.

The road got worse the farther north they traveled. Not only was it muddy, but the cavalry had to ford two streams that crossed the trail. Along the way, tempers flared as Castleton, Connors, and Marshall engaged in a heated discussion. Each had his own opinion about the best route east to avoid Confederate patrols.

Because the woodsman was the most belligerent, his argument won in the end. "We *must* go to Driftwood," Connors insisted. "We can build rafts there and float down to Harrisburg."

"But we still don't know the purpose of this here goose chase," grumbled Marshall.

"I'm just following orders like you," declared Castleton, avoiding the sergeant's eyes.

"The way we's guardin' this hay, you'd think it was spun gold!"

Hot and sweaty, the Union Cavalry pulled into Ridgway around suppertime. Many of the citizens were *drinking* their dinners and spilled into the street to curse the arriving Yanks. As the hostile crowd rushed to surround the wagon, Castleton yelled, "Looks like Copperheads aren't only crawling in the woods. Draw your pistols, men!"

"But how could these Reb lovers come to a town that sent us so many good Bucktails?" wondered Marshall.

Connors mumbled something under his breath and then winked at a demonstrator in the front row. Ignoring Castleton's command, his pistol stayed snapped in its holster.

When the Copperheads didn't disperse as ordered, the lieutenant fired a shot over their heads to part the mob. Although darkness was falling fast, the caravan fled toward St. Marys.

The Yanks hadn't gone far before the mugginess of the night brought back Castleton's fever. In the throes of his delirium, he confessed the secrets of their mission. The mouths of his soldiers flew open in disbelief as they snatched the carbines from their saddles. Forming a tight formation around the wagon, they rode with their senses alert for danger.

At first light, the soldiers had a meeting and then demanded to see the gold. The lieutenant was in no condition to resist as they unloaded him with the hay bales along the roadside.

"Shucks, this ain't gold at all!" cried one trooper after the false bottom had been pulled from the wagon.

"Let me take a look," said Connors, drawing a knife from his pocket. A low whistle escaped from the men at the glistening scratch he made in one of the painted bars.

"I best ride ahead and check the trail for ambushers," Connors said after ogling the gold with hungry eyes.

"And weaken our force even further?" cried Marshall. "The lieutenant can't even sit up, let alone fire a pistol. We need everyone right here to de-fend this treasure."

"You forget that I'm in charge, Sergeant. If I run into trouble, I'll gallop back to warn you. In the meantime, mount up and stay close to the wagon."

The cavalry traveled the rest of the night without incident. Connors finally returned when they reached the outskirts of St. Marys. There, they were greeted as heroes with a waving of flags and a free meal prepared by the Dutch dames of the village. Other gals healed their loneliness for a few greenbacks. The mission was delayed for a full day while the lieutenant drank medicine and the cavalry were "doctored" by the young women.

Rested and grinning, the troopers departed from St. Marys. Their merriment soon vanished when the skies opened to flood the streams and block the wagon's passage. Adding to their troubles, the lieutenant grew terribly ill. Ravaged by fever, he gave up the ghost while they slogged down a rain-drenched road.

After burying Castleton, Connors ordered the party onto the trail to Caledonia. It was the last route open, so the soldiers could do nothing but obey.

"If this ain't a frog strangler, I ain't never seen one," murmured Sergeant Marshall as the rain fell in buckets.

"We shoulda buried the dang gold with the lieutenant," muttered another soaked trooper. "We won't spend a nickel of it nohow."

The cavalry sloshed along, drenched to the skin through their blue coats. This was boggy country, and their mounts clopped over corduroy roads built through a series of swamps. Just before reaching solid ground, they spied a rock formation looming from the ridge ahead.

Connors, who led the column, dug his spurs into his horse's flanks. Hell-bent-for-leather, he galloped howling up the rise. He had just disappeared when the Yankees were strafed by gunfire from the rocks. Two troopers were killed in the first barrage while two others were blasted from the saddle clutching their shoulders. The sergeant dove under the wagon and used a wheel for cover. The driver was the next to fall, and he flopped in the mud bleeding from his neck and head.

Marshall smoothed his mustache and calmly searched for a target. He didn't have to look long before he saw a tall bushwhacker creeping ahead through the rocks. He was dressed like a lumberman in a red flannel shirt and tall boots. Although bowed at the waist, he wasn't as sneaky as he thought. The sergeant shot him squarely through the chest and then worked the lever of his Spencer carbine to load another round.

Although vastly outnumbered, the cavalry fought with the fury of cornered men. For an hour they held out as bullets whined past or thudded into the dead horses they hid behind. Their Spencers cracked repeatedly, and their accurate aim drove back the bushwhackers again and again. When their rifles clicked empty, they drew their pistols and continued the fight. Twenty bloody bodies littered the woods before they in turn were annihilated.

When Sergeant Marshall was the last one alive, he remembered the purpose of their mission. "Cripes alfriday!" he growled. "No way am I gonna let these weasels steal the Union's gold. Don't matter if they're Rebs, Copperheads, or just plain thieves. All I know fer sure is that Connors led us into this trap. Let 'im burn in hell before he pilfers one bar!"

Scrambling from under the wagon, Marshall leaped into the seat and snatched up a whip. He lashed it near the mules' ears to get them moving. The animals hadn't been shot because they were needed to carry the treasure from this hellish tangle.

As slugs sang past the sergeant's face, he urged the mules off into the bog. They flailed their legs and plunged ahead until up to their bellies in muck. He usually cursed the stupidly of these beasts, but now it worked in his favor. The wagon lurched from the corduroy road and sank in the gurgling mire. Marshall rode the gold to the bottom. A bullet ended his heroics when he popped like a frog to the surface.

Connors galloped his horse down to the edge of the swamp. After howling in frustration, he yelped, "Knew I should have bribed that sergeant."

"Wouldn'ta done no good," drawled the head bandit. "Shoulda *killed him* along the trail."

"Well, we've lost all the gold thanks to that saint!" cried Connors, emptying his revolver into Marshall's floating corpse.

"An' I lost half o' my best men fer nothin'! It looks like it's *you* who'll have ta pay now."

"What do you mean? I don't have any money."

"Ya got a horse, a pistol, an' a brand new rifle."

"But how will I get home?"

"Walk."

"In a wilderness full of rattlers and catamounts? Without weapons?"

"We'd shoot ya, but that'd be too good fer a skunk like you. Ya best git movin', Connors. If we catch ya after we bury our boys, all bets are off."

"But I cut you in on a sweet deal. We were going to be rich!"

"Sure. By sellin' out your own troopers. Now, we're turnin' on you, pard."

Guarding Lincoln

As Corporal Colby Tupper stared out the window of the moving train, scenes from bloody Gettysburg replayed in his head. Exploding shells rained around him. Howling Rebs advanced across a field. Barked commands, a counterattack, Colonel Wister's bloody face. He stood behind a fence. Firin' 'til his rifle was too hot to hold. Then, the ground rose up to meet him. . .

Three strident blasts from the engine whistle returned Tupper to reality. He found himself covered with sweat and unbuttoned his frock coat to cool down. Atop his knee, he gripped a Union cap adorned with a buck tail and, in gold numbers and letters, 150 PV, Co. K.

The train pulled up to a depot, and Corporal Tupper descended into the bustling city of Washington. He was greeted by another soldier wearing a bucktailed cap and was led to a waiting buckboard. The corporal still walked with a limp but needed no help from his escort to climb into the wagon. The private did fetch Tupper's bags for him, though, and placed them in the back.

The buckboard clattered down a rutted dirt street that led to the northern suburbs of the city. After three bumpy miles, it arrived at the Soldiers' Home. This was a collection of stone buildings that housed disabled soldiers and their attending staff. A short distance away stood a mansion that President Lincoln used for his summer home.

As Tupper watched amputees with crutches and in wheelchairs, he realized how close he had come to joining the Invalid Corps. At least he was still fit to stand guard duty and fire a weapon if needed. Bowing his head, he thanked God for healing his battle wounds.

Tupper followed the private to a military encampment. It was nestled in an oak grove near the mansion. He had just stashed his gear in his tent when he was told to report to Captain Derickson at headquarters.

Derickson had a neatly trimmed moustache and a friendly air about him. Despite his likable qualities, there was no doubt that he was in command. After eyeing the corporal up and down he said, "It's Mr. Lincoln's custom to meet all the new men assigned here. Return at six a.m. We'll breakfast with the President, so he can get to know you."

With a surprised gulp, Tupper saluted. Afterward, he croaked, "Yes, sir!"

"And be prompt, Corporal. The President doesn't like to be kept waiting."

When the Bucktails arrived at the mansion the next morning, Lincoln was busy reading from the scriptures. "I find Psalm 50 fascinating, don't you, Captain?" he said when they entered. "'The mighty God, even the Lord, hath spoken, and called the earth from the rising of the sun unto the going down thereof. Out of Zion, the perfection of beauty, God hath shined. Our God shall come, and shall not keep silence: a fire shall devour before him, and it shall be tempestuous round him. He shall call to the heavens from above, and to the earth, that he may judge his people.' "

"And on that day, Robert E. Lee will surrender his Philistines," replied Derickson with a grin.

"Who do we have here?" asked Lincoln, nodding toward the corporal. "Please come and sit."

"I'm Colby Tupper, Mr. President, of the 150th Bucktail Regiment. I arrived last night to join your bodyguard."

"You mean my *boys*, don't you, son? Where are you from? I imagine Pennsylvania."

"From Eldred, Pennsylvania, to be exact, sir. My father is William and my ma, Jerusha."

"Well, I hope the vittles my cooks serve this morning will measure up to those of your good mother."

"I'm sure they will, sir."

After breakfast, Derickson and Tupper rode with the President to the White House in his carriage. They were accompanied by a detachment of Ohio cavalry. There were two more mounted guards at the entrance of the estate and a dismounted sergeant posted near the front door. Once inside, Tupper didn't spot another sentry. When he saw that the whole East Wing was unoccupied except for a messenger, he said, "Excuse me, Mr. Lincoln, but shouldn't you have guards near your office, too?"

"Now, you sound like Mother," chuckled the President. "She got a notion in her head that I shall be assassinated. To please her, I take a cane when I go to the War Department at night — when I don't forget it."

With such an affable man to look after, Tupper enjoyed his bodyguard duties. The other Bucktails were of like mind because the President took a personal interest in each of them. It was his custom in the evenings to drop by their camp and inquire if the men were comfortable. On Christmas, accompanied by Mrs. Lincoln, he said they were part of his family — and meant it!

There was one Bucktail, though, who wanted to be transferred to a combat unit. Tupper was in the President's office when the soldier stormed through

Misdeeds & Misadventures

the door. After listening to his pleas to be sent off to battle, Lincoln cleared his throat and murmured, "You remind me of a farmer friend of mine in Illinois, who said he could never understand why the Lord put a curl in a pig's tail. It never seemed to him to be either useful or ornamental, but he reckoned that the Almighty knew what he was doing when he put it there. It is a soldier's duty to obey orders without question. You are serving your country as faithfully here as at the front, and I reckon it is pleasanter and safer here than there. Now, return to your quarters, Private."

One man Lincoln couldn't dissuade from leaving was Captain Derickson, who resigned to become Provost Marshal of Pennsylvania's Twentieth District. After the captain's departure, Tupper drew even more assignments to accompany the President on his comings and goings through Washington. With the strain of conducting the war in its fifth year, the corporal worried about Lincoln. With each passing day, he grew paler and spoke of nightmares where he saw himself dead.

News of the Union victory at Appomattox Court House finally lifted the President's spirits. To celebrate, he and Mrs. Lincoln attended Ford's Theater to watch *Our American Cousin*. Corporal Tupper was guarding one of the entrances and saw the Lincolns arrive late. They hurried inside and had just settled into the Presidential Box when the play was stopped. As the orchestra performed "Hail to the Chief," the audience roared its approval. The applause returned to laughter once the comedy resumed.

Corporal Tupper fidgeted at his post. He could smell danger, and the reek of it surrounded Ford's Theater. He, too, had had nightmares. His were of copperheads coiled beneath his bed waiting to bite him. He could taste their venom and hear their horrible hissing. The dreams were so real that he slept with his pistol three nights running.

Tupper remained on high alert, his pulse thudding in his temples. Why had a policeman been assigned to guard Lincoln's box when so many Bucktails were ready to lay down their lives for him? This thought had barely entered his mind when he saw that very cop entering a tavern across the street with the President's coachman. It was now intermission, and the stream of playgoers demanded Tupper's full attention.

After twenty minutes, *Our American Cousin* resumed again, and ladies' titter and gentlemen's guffaws announced that the play was a success. During the height of the ovation, Tupper swore he heard a gunshot. He ripped open the door and rushed up the nearest aisle with his rifle ready. He saw a man leap from the Presidential Box, land awkwardly on the stage, and then limp across it as if part of the show. Waving a bloody knife over his head, he bellowed, "The South is avenged!"

Still wide-eyed with surprise, the corporal heard someone yell from above, "Stop that man!" Before he could get off a shot, the actor exited a side door and disappeared. Then, Tupper was surrounded by hysteria as Mrs. Lincoln's screams cascaded over the railing.

"Good Lord, the President's been shot!" cried a well-dressed young man, pushing his way toward the balcony staircase. Tupper recognized him as Charles Leale, the same army surgeon who had treated his wounds. Following the doctor up the stairs, he found the door to the Presidential Box jammed shut. With a vicious kick, Tupper opened it and then assisted Leale as he examined Abe Lincoln.

Leale ripped off the President's blood-soaked collar. Then, he opened Abe's shirt to improve his breathing. Next, he felt around the back of Lincoln's head until he found a wound next to his left ear. The bullet was too deep to remove and had burrowed through the left side of the brain to lodge above his right eye.

Tupper felt sick when he saw brains leaking from the President's head. He snatched the murder weapon from the floor and felt its heat in his hand. He saw that it was a Philadelphia Derringer only accurate to a few feet. He surmised that the killer pressed the barrel against Lincoln's head when he fired it. Scorched hair and a powder burn confirmed his suspicions.

Leale loosened a clot of blood from the President's wound, and he breathed a little better. He had not regained consciousness, though, and the surgeon figured the end was near. "His wound is mortal," he announced, sniffing back tears. "Let's get him out of here."

Two more doctors had joined Leale. Together with Tupper and another soldier, they carried the President down the stairs and out the front door of Ford's Theater. Across the street, a dark figure was holding a lantern and urged the men to bring Lincoln into his boarding house. Inside, they laid their bleeding patient diagonally across the bed because he wouldn't fit lengthwise.

Corporal Tupper returned outside and stood guard all night with soldiers who came scrambling up the street. When Secretary Stanton emerged from the house the next morning, he said, "Now, he belongs to the angels." None of the horror the corporal had witnessed at Gettysburg could compare to losing Lincoln. Openly, he wept.

Because of his devotion to the President, Colby Tupper was chosen as one of the honor guards who watched over Lincoln's body in the Capitol Rotunda. He touched the bill of his Bucktail cap in a final salute before returning to his duties at the Soldiers' Home. Another President now lived there. One who needed vigilant protection.

In Pairs

Jim crept stealthily up the point of a hemlock-choked hill. He followed an eroded lease road flanked by gloomy rooms of trees. The skies churned with clouds as the threat of snow grew by the minute. Six inches of snow was already on the ground and coated the orange leaves of dense beech brush.

The hunter paused to catch his breath. The grade was a steep one, and his brawny chest heaved with his upward climb. He wore camo clothes and heavy insulated boots. In the crook of his arm he carried a scoped rifle.

Jim had been laid off from his construction job all hunting season. Being in the woods every day had fine-tuned his senses, and he listened and watched like an animal. Not one bird chirp or rustling of the branches escaped him as he scanned the surrounding hillside. Three other times he had run across flocks of turkeys in this same area, and he knew they would still be combing these thickets for the ample crop of beechnuts that they loved.

The last time Jim came here, he was armed with his shotgun. The twelve gauge loaded with number four shot was only effective to forty yards, and the flock he encountered was a hundred yards away. Even after he had busted them up, he couldn't call the varmints back within shotgun range. Only when he returned home did he learn why. Son of a bitch! He had forgotten to flip his orange cap to the camouflage side while working his slate call.

The time before that, he had his 30.06 when he flushed two hens from the top of a tree. They had flown right over his head, but a rifle was useless for a wing shot. And his other confrontation? Why, of course, he was lugging his shotgun only to see two big gobblers strutting off across a field.

Remembering these frustrations, Jim muttered, "Wish I had an over-and-under, by damn! A .222 over a twelve gauge would be just the ticket. Then, they wouldn't outsmart me, the dirty buggers!"

With a determined scowl, the hunter continued up the hill until he came to a fork in the road. There, he sneaked to the right and peered into a valley below. He stood frozen for fifteen minutes watching for the telltale movement of bobbing bird heads. When nothing moved but wind-tossed trees, he returned to the road that ran to the top of a steep mountain.

Jim continued his climb until he reached a dim trail that wound around the hillside to the left. Moving one careful step at a time, he entered a beech thicket that had been scratched to pieces on every hunt he had made into this hollow. He had only crept a short ways when he heard the cluck of hens and a frantic scraping.

Jim clicked his .06 off safe and raised it to his shoulder. He took two more stealthy steps before spotting several black shapes working through the brush ahead. The birds were so busy feasting on beechnuts that they paid him no heed. Their red and blue heads nodded busily to peck at the food their clawed feet dug from snow and leaves.

The hunter stared through his scope and then adjusted it from four to six power to better see the limbs that obstructed his aim. Even a twig would blow up an .06 bullet, so he waited for a clear shot.

The longer Jim stood, the shakier the gun got in his hands. The hens would not stand still, and the gobblers stayed hidden in the brush. He'd only get one shot before the flock scattered, so he *had* to be patient. He never did find an opening to shoot through as the turkeys worked into denser growth.

When the last bird disappeared uphill, Jim cursed under his breath. It was then that it began to snow — hard. Assailed by the blizzard, the hunter shivered and coughed into his hand. He couldn't see farther than ten yards in any direction, so he figured his best bet was to circle above his prey and let them come to him.

With that purpose in mind, Jim veered off to the right and scrambled onto the road that ran up the spine of the mountain. He didn't care how loudly his footsteps crunched, for the turkeys were now out of hearing.

Jim jogged up the snowy road until he reached the hemlock-crowned peak. There, he stopped and took ten deep breaths. After wiping sweat from his forehead, he slipped through the trees to watch the bench below. He carefully concealed himself behind a tree trunk and pointed his rifle barrel down the hill.

The snow was still falling fast, and the hunter's clothes were white with it. He began to tremble with cold and anticipation as he wondered what had become of the turkeys. This is where they should have come, judging by their habits and the lay of the land.

As Jim emitted an impatient sigh, he caught a glimpse of what resembled a lost dog. It was heavy with winter fur and loped along sniffing the air with purpose. Although large as a German shepherd, it was mainly gray in color. Unlike a normal pooch, it kept its tail down as it moved through the brush.

Jim was so surprised by the canine's appearance that he didn't think to peer at it through his scope until it had nearly disappeared into a grove of trees. He had heard of coyote sightings by other hunters but had not experienced one — until now!

The dirty bugger must be huntin' them turkeys like me, thought Jim. *Boy, was he a big brute!*

Jim waited a full five minutes before creeping down the hillside to examine the tracks of the beast. Each huge footprint was elongated and had four toes tipped by sharp claws. He gasped at the size of the tracks and then muttered, "This must be a wolf-coyote hybrid Dad heard were released by the game commission. The jerk-offs already let fishers loose. Soon, there'll be more predators than grouse an' turkey in these woods. I best see if I can hunt the rascal down."

Now, completely covered with snow, Jim moved like a wraith along the coyote's trail. He looked warily ahead as he slipped along until his exhaled breath fogged his glasses. He had just wiped them clean with his handkerchief when he spotted the canine skulking through the woods in front of him.

Jim snapped his rifle to his shoulder, causing his prey to freeze in its tracks. Instead of loping off, the beast turned with a snarl and charged. It zigzagged through goldenrod and leaped over stumps as it rushed him. The hunter couldn't keep it in his scope long enough to squeeze off a shot. When it closed within fifteen yards, frothing and snapping its jaws, Jim fired anyway. The bullet struck the ground between the beast's feet, spraying it with snow and frozen earth. With a surprised yip, it leaped over a nearby bank and disappeared.

Jim was quivering all over. He had never heard of a coyote attacking a man. Was this one rabid, or did it mistake him for a turkey? *I am covered with snow*, he reasoned. *Ain't got a human shape no more.*

With an angry growl, the hunter slapped the snow from his coat. He broke into a string of curses when he brushed off his hat and knocked cold, white powder down his neck.

"Just my stinkin' luck," fumed Jim, staring at the .06 clutched in his hands. "Brought the wrong gun again. Why, a load of number four's woulda blowed half his head off, the dirty cuss! Damn him anyhow!"

Jim tried ejecting his spent cartridge. He found his rifle bolt frozen shut. As he frantically tugged and jerked at it, he spied a gray beast crouched behind a log.

The hunter emitted a fearful cry. Running would not save him, and there was no tree close enough to climb. As he brandished his rifle like a club, the first coyote boiled up over the bank and lunged for him. Jim had heard they hunted in pairs. Now, he learned firsthand the sharpness of their fangs and claws.

The Chasm

As a Gemini, I hate being bored. After enduring two days of constant rain that confined me to my house, I loaded some fishing gear into the Jeep and headed off to my favorite brown trout stream. Brownies go on a feeding frenzy when roily water rises, so I left with high hopes.

The windshield wipers worked overtime on my half-hour drive through another downpour. Roadside ditches flowed with muddy runoff, and water pooled everywhere in fields and lawns. The highway wasn't flooded, though, so I took that as a good sign.

When I reached the creek, I emitted a deep groan. The water had risen to the top of the banks and still hadn't crested. There was no way to tell where one pool ended and the next began, inundated by the muddy tide. It wouldn't matter how many sinkers I attached to my line. My bait wouldn't stay submerged in this roaring torrent.

The stubborn Scotsman I am, I pulled on my cap and waders and then wormed into my fishing vest. Snatching up my spinning rod, I tramped upstream until I reached a feeder creek. It wasn't nearly as wild as the flood it spewed into and looked pretty fishable.

Flashing a grin, I moved up the side valley that was choked with dripping hemlocks. Everywhere, clumps of ferns sprouted from the black soil and grabbed at my legs as I waded through them. This stream flowed across an abandoned oil field, and silent jacks and pieces of rusted pipe provided a reminder of the boom days of yore. As I stomped along, I was thankful that the rain had put down the gnats that usually attacked me when I entered these woods.

I opened my bait box and snipped a night crawler in half. I threaded the light half on a number eight hook. I used ultralight equipment to get the most action from the scrappy trout I sought. My four pound test line made fighting these fish even trickier and gave them every advantage to break off and escape.

I clamped three split shot four inches above the hook and cast my bait into the first hole I came to. The water was murky, so sneaking to the stream was unnecessary. When my line drifted past a submerged rock, it came to a sudden stop. I lifted my rod and felt the thump, thump of a biting trout. I dropped my rod tip and waited a few seconds. When I struck at the fish, it was gone.

I reeled in my worm and found one end of it gnawed off. "Dang!" I muttered. "Missed 'im!"

Tossing my bait back into the creek, I repeated the same drift with no luck. Disgusted, I reeled in my line and moved on to the next hole. There, another fish bumped the worm but didn't take it. The same thing happened in the third hole, too.

"Lots of food washed in with this rain," I grumbled. "The trout must be full!"

I had reached a deep run that wasn't as swift as the other places I had fished. Attaching a whole night crawler, I cast it to the head of the run and let it roll along the bottom until it came to an abrupt halt. Tightening my line, I felt it vibrate with the weight of a heavy fish. I immediately set the hook and was fast to a brownie that flashed its bronze side and then tore off upstream. My pole bent double beneath the strain and did nothing to stop the fish's flight. In desperation, I tugged too hard, and the line snapped with a sickening twang.

My heart was pounding with excitement when I reeled in my broken line. I dug another hook from my vest, but my trembling fingers wouldn't tie it on. Just then, the sun broke through the clouds. Warmed by the bright rays, I rigged up my line and entered the deeper forest ahead.

Here, the hemlocks formed a thick canopy over the creek. The banks of the valley steepened, too, and I found myself in a chasm strewn with rocks. Water roared in this gorge like an angered bear, and my ears rang with its fury. One waterfall followed another, and I was awed by the wild beauty of the place. When a fresh rainstorm hit, it got so black I could barely see to cast. At the darkest point, I caught two browns in quick succession.

After cleaning the trout, I clambered up a bank and descended next to a gurgling pool. Casting into it, my worm barely sank when a hard hit nearly wrenched the pole from my hands. This fish meant business. It dug deep and then exploded to the surface to thrash and roll. When that didn't work, it swam downstream in a mad rush that had me scrambling over slick rocks to keep up. Now, the brown was below me, and my heart sank as it opened its mouth and violently shook its dark head. Somehow, the hook held, so I played the monster up to the bank. I quickly pounced on it and broke its neck.

Now, I had three trout to eat for dinner but needed more for the ninety-two-year-old neighbor lady. She had a young outlook and the appetite to match. She was a true inspiration for more than just catching fish.

The going got tougher as the chasm narrowed. The banks were straight up and down and pinched the creek between them in a series of rapids and foaming falls. I had trouble keeping my balance on the wet rocks and even more problems climbing over boulders. When the terrain got too rough, I was forced to wade up the creek. Thus positioned, I cast into a pothole and hooked an acrobatic brown. It jumped and splashed atop the water all the way to my boots where it spit out the hook and streaked away.

Finally, the stream leveled out again, and I saw where a pipeline crossed it. Just below the pipeline was a pool full of submerged rocks. I flipped my worm into a swirling backwash and watched wide-eyed as a black shape attacked it. I pulled back on my rod and was fast to another little cannibal that scrapped and splashed and tugged. After several minutes, I dragged it up on a sandbar where it continued to flop and fight.

Next, I entered an upper gorge that was steeper than the one below. The creek was wilder here, too, and whitewater rapids predominated. I managed to catch my final fish by drifting a worm beneath an undercut bank. The brown hit so hard that I didn't have to set the hook. It swallowed the bait down to its gullet.

With my limit caught, I wondered if I should climb the treacherous hillside to the road above. It seemed better than wading downstream over ankle-busting rocks. As I glanced around to get my bearings, the sky suddenly darkened, and raindrops pattered on the bill of my cap. I felt like Rip Van Winkle when thunder caromed off the walls of the chasm.

William P. Robertson

Each Summer Writes
Its Own Story

Each summer writes its own story. 1967 was no exception. That year our family vacationed at Millsite Lake near the Thousand Islands, New York, and a squirrely kid named Rocky stayed in the cottage next door. Dad said he was a "juvenile delinquent," but I just thought he was nuts.

On a muggy afternoon, we took Rocky fishing. We rowed out to the far edge of the weed bed in front of our camp to drown a few worms. It was so hot that even the sunfish weren't biting. Rocky got very frustrated watching his bobber float merrily across the waves. It never dipped once in an hour's time. Finally, he stood up, bellowed a cuss word, and leaped from the boat with a wild scream. When he hit the water, his scream became more urgent. He couldn't swim a lick in the biker boots he forgot to shed before jumping overboard.

Another day I was fishing off the dock, flinging a Pikie Minnow with my bait casting rod. I could throw the lure fifty yards if the line didn't snarl up in my open face reel. That happened about every third cast. While I cleared one of those "bird nests," I didn't hear Rocky creeping up behind me until he emitted his braying laugh.

The Pikie Minnow had three sets of treble hooks that were razor sharp. When I started casting it again, I warned Rocky to keep back. He listened about as well as he swam and edged closer with each cast I made. He also insulted my fishing technique. His criticism made me hurl my lure harder. I kept telling him to stay away, but he was like an insect buzzing near flypaper.

Suddenly, I had a sharp strike. It startled me so much that I missed the fish. Angrily, I reeled in the Pikie Minnow and then tried flipping it to where I got the hit. I moved my rod backward and snapped my wrist to shoot the line ahead. Instead of the nice smooth cast I envisioned, my arm came to an abrupt stop. I heard a yelp behind me and turned to see my lure snagged in the zipper of Rocky's pants. His mouth was frozen open in an O of horror. His eyes were real big!

Needless to say, that was the last time Rocky came onto the dock to "coach" me. After his boots shrank too small for him to wear them, he spent the rest of his vacation catchin' rays on the beach. Naturally, he blasted '60's punk from his transistor radio to bug the other sunbathers.

Misdeeds & Misadventures

BLACKBIRDS

A motorcyclist roared up a dirt road, leaving a broad trail of dust in his wake. He wore the uniform of a local messenger service, complete with a dark vest and a tweed cap. He had a stern look on his long Irish face, and goggles masked his deadly eyes.

The man was Paul "the Trigger" Walsh. He cleaned up "messes" for the Black Hand, and most of the corpses that floated down the creek through town were his handiwork. Of course, those were just thugs and two-bit gangsters, so the coppers didn't do much to investigate their extermination.

Now, Paul was to "rub out" the judge who had queered his boss. Like any true professional, he had tailed this judge through two weeks' activities and found him a strict creature of habit. His house was just up the way, and Paul had to be there at precisely seven a.m.

Squealing around a corner, Paul pulled up beside a mailbox just as the judge, clad only in a bathrobe, reached inside to retrieve his morning paper. When he saw the "messenger" approach, he held out his hand. He was expecting a congratulatory letter that should have come yesterday. It was from the governor for convicting John Musolino to a life sentence in the slammer.

Instead of an envelope, Paul pulled a Luger from his pouch. Coolly, he planted one bullet in the middle of the judge's forehead. He roared his motor just as he shot to hide the noise of the muzzle blast.

Paul slung the judge's limp body over his handlebars and sped off in a covering cloud of dust. Sticking to the side roads, he headed for a secluded landfill near Lafayette. He arrived there without passing another vehicle and circled to the back of the dump. That's where he had deposited some fresh deer carcasses, and they bore the signs of recent feedings.

While Paul heaved the judge's body next to the dead deer, he saw a pair of turkey buzzards circling above. The squawk of crows echoed from a nearby thicket, as well. Paul was most pleased when he saw a swarm of blackbirds descend from the sky. As vicious as he, they pecked heads into unrecognizable skulls.

The Gangster

Buffalo Al strutted into the speakeasy dressed in his flashiest suit. He wore a striped blue jacket with matching pants and a blue vest coated with steel to deflect bullets. He had a Colt pistol in a shoulder holster tucked under his armpit and two Lugers stuffed in his belt. Al's smile beamed with confidence and charisma. Every dame in the joint marked his entrance.

Al sat in a booth facing the dance floor. His dark eyes glittered as he watched the flappers shake their asses to "Everything Is Hotsy Totsy Now." He was soon joined by Joe Morbito and Francesco Colella, who wore matching black fedoras and wingtip shoes. Their breath smelled of hooch, and their speech was slurred when they ordered glasses of rum. Joe already looked fried to the hat.

"Where's Flo?" asked Colella as he ogled a passing Sheba.

"She threw me over. Ain't ya heard? She's Rinaldi's moll now."

"You mean that thug whose joint got closed by the coppers?"

"Don't know nothing about that," Al said with a wink.

"Well, you best watch your back," cautioned Joe, "even if you are the big cheese."

"Got that covered," replied the gangster, unbuttoning his coat to reveal the twin Lugers. "The hell with Rinaldi. Let's find us some dolls and make whoopee. Look at the chassis on that one!"

Al opened his wallet and flashed a big wad of dough. After he bought two rounds for the house, he had a dame on each arm and another sitting on his lap. The whole booth was crawling with dames, and Al's hands were as busy as his flattering tongue. Colella and Morbito were pushed aside and staggered off grumbling to the bar.

A little after eleven, Al left the speakeasy reeking of perfume. His pulse still pounded with lust, and the liquor he swilled made him quite zozzled. He strode up to his yellow roadster parked along the street. He gave it a loving pat while climbing behind the wheel. The car was a real breezer, and Al thought about putting down the top to cool off on the ride home. Before he could do so, a black sedan pulled up on his back bumper and blinded him with its headlights.

"What the hell?" cussed Al, whirling around in his seat. "Scram, ya bums!"

There were two loud blasts, and the inside of Al's car buzzed as though full of bees. It was also alive with flying glass as the windshield exploded from the shots that followed. He yelped in sudden pain when his shoulder and face felt like pins had pricked them.

Diving on the passenger side floor, Al fumbled for his pistols. A squeal of tires accompanied the assassins' sedan as it pulled alongside to rake him with more buckshot. By then, he held a Luger in each hand and fired wildly out the side window. He blazed away until the car screeched off and his magazines were empty.

The gangster was now aware that he was leaking blood. Tossing aside the pistols, he gripped the dashboard, cutting his hands on shards of glass. Yelping with pain, he reached for the steering wheel and pulled himself up. He yanked out the Colt revolver before lurching to his feet.

Through blurry eyes, Al saw a red light down the street. Thinking it signified a brothel, he swayed toward it. On the way, he fell twice on the brick pavement. Finally, he reached the door and turned the knob clumsily until it opened. As he collapsed inside, he found himself in the Olean firehouse surrounded by uniformed men.

"I've been shot," Al gasped. "Help me."

"Look at how much he's bleeding, Floyd! Call an ambulance!"

"Ab-so-lute-ly!"

Al woke up the next morning in the hospital with his shoulder, neck, and face heavily bandaged. His bed was surrounded by anxious men in suits. Along with Colella and Morbito, the Mussare brothers from Buffalo stared down at him.

"You had a close call, boss," mumbled Joe. "Them bums was armed with sawed-off shotguns that the coppers found in a trash barrel this morning."

"Did you see who shot you?" asked Fred Mussare, patting Al sympathetically on the arm.

"Rinaldi," said Al in a hoarse whisper. "I'm sure."

"Then, we know what to do. . ."

"And kill that conniving bitch, Flo, while you're at it. If it weren't for her, I wouldn't be laying here shot full of holes."

Finger And Thumb

Me and Stevie had the worst jobs in the plant. We spent all night bent over a wheel buffin' knife blades 'til our fingers got cramped to shit. We got cut to shit, too! All for a week's vacation you could use a day at a time.

We played lots of music trivia, we did. How did 10cc get their name? Who was the first rock star to expose himself on stage? Who sang "You're Breakin' My Heart, You're Tearin' It Apart, So F--- You?"

We got stoned every night at lunch. You bet! Then, Stevie smoked doobies in the john, sittin' in the last stall under a ceiling vent. I sat on the next shitter checkin' out drawings by the plant artist. They taught me *all* about the female body!

We joked about poppin' a finger for some real down time. An' a fat disability check instead of eight bucks an hour. Yeah, right until Stevie went and done it. One minute he was askin', "Who wrote 'Atomic Dog'?" The next, his finger and thumb lay between us like uncooked sausages.

Man, the foreman had a bird! Bitched all the way to the hospital 'bout his safety record bein' in the shitter. He screamed for a urinalysis. Impaired employees weren't his responsibility. You bet! So what if Stevie never worked again?

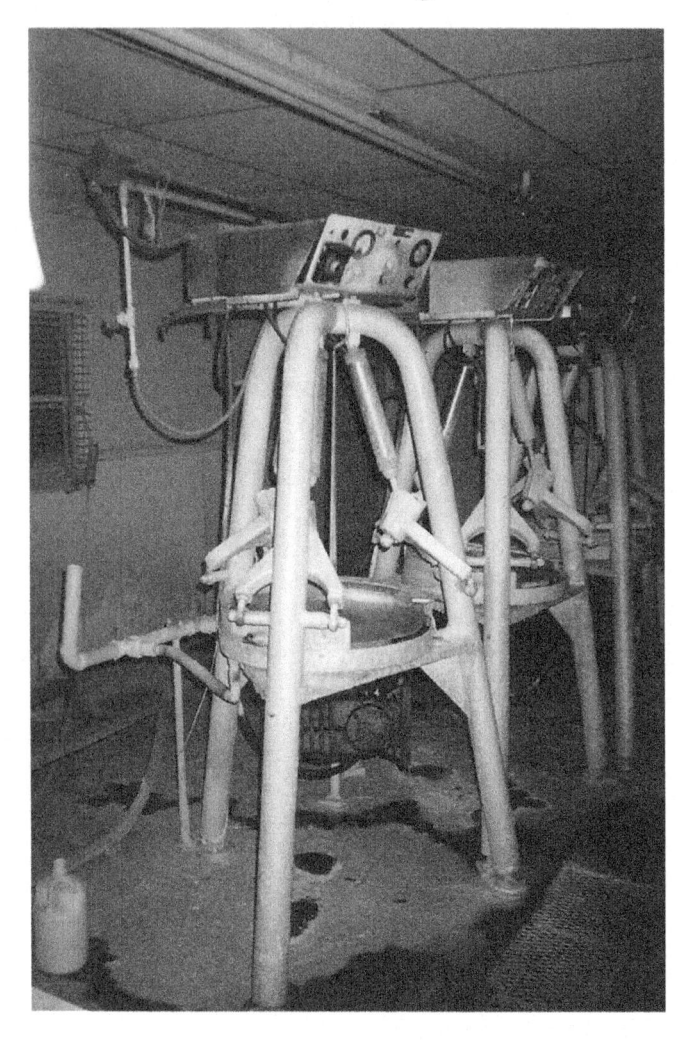

Goosey

One summer to make money for college, I worked as a rough grinder in a factory. Armed with a chipping hammer, I gouged slag off metal rings that were used to fit huge oil pipes together. Half the guys in my department had fingers missing. The rest were half out of their minds.

Luckily, I got along with everyone. They said I was on the "gravy train" going to MU, and all. I laughed at their kidding, did what I was told, and otherwise kept my mouth shut.

The foreman's name was Cal. He was a strong, likeable guy who ran a really loose ship. As long as you showed up every night and punched in on time, he gave you no grief. He liked joking around as much as his workers and turned a blind eye to the pranks they pulled.

Most of the pranks were played on Himes. He was a hyper dude who chain-smoked cigarettes all night. His nervousness was intensified by the Coke he guzzled. Man, he kept the soda vendor in business all by himself.

When the guys in the department learned Himes was goosey, they declared open season on him.

They constantly dropped clanging metal beside him just to see him come unglued. And every time the chump bent over, someone shoved a broom handle up his butt. Instead of fighting back, he yelped and cried and caterwauled and bounced off the walls like a rubber ball.

Himes' two biggest tormentors were Bud and Joe. They were overweight former football players who were once superstars at the local high school. They both had been named to the All-State Team, had gotten full rides to prominent colleges, and then promptly flunked out. Now, instead of blocking linebackers, they wrestled hunks of steel around all night. They had failed life miserably, so they doled out their own form of misery to Himes.

One night Himes came to work hungover. His eyes were glassy, and his face was white as chalk. With callous sneers, Bud and Joe followed him into the restroom.

Himes had just turned on a faucet to splash cold water on himself when Bud said, "I shouldn'ta ate them leftovers before comin' tonight."

"Why not?" asked Joe on cue.

"'Cause I-I-I'm gonna puke!"

Bud bent over a nearby toilet and gagged so loud that he drown out the whine of two grinders. He continued his theatrics until Himes turned around to see if he was okay. Just then, Bud emptied a can of soup into the john. The vegetables and beef looked like his lost lunch, and Himes vomited for real. A torrent of green slime shot from his mouth and splattered through the doorway just as Cal entered. Himes spent the rest of the night cleaning every inch of the restroom and the vile toilet Bud later shit all over.

From then on, Himes' tormentors heckled him with a fury. One night they knocked him off a ladder and then shut him up in his locker to scream for an hour. They released him just in time for supper. When he found the catsup-soaked Kotex they'd put in his dinner pail, he shrieked like a schoolgirl and ran barfing out the door.

Each atrocity made Himes shake worse. He also became more accident-prone. In three successive nights he burned himself with a blowtorch, tripped and sprained his ankle, and hammered his thumb flat. Of course, every time he bent over, there was Bud to goose him with a broom handle and Joe to shout, "Klutz!"

Friday was no different. After putting a rat in Himes' locker, Bud planned the coup de grace. He concealed himself in a trash barrel by closing the flaps of a box over his head. After he was hidden, Joe dropped a candy wrapper and bullied Himes into throwing it away. When the poor sap chucked it in the barrel, Bud burst out like a jack-in-the-box yelling at the top of his lungs. Himes' face contorted with fear, and he leaped three feet in the air. He hit the floor running with Joe's mocking laughter ringing in his ears.

"I never get tired of pickin' on that wimp!" howled Bud.

"Neither do I," guffawed Joe. "That's the last we'll see of him 'til Monday."

The words were barely out of Joe's mouth when he turned to watch Himes rush back into the department. He was gibbering like an ape and had a rivet gun clutched in his right hand. He snapped the gun onto an air hose and began spraying rivets everywhere. They pinged off lockers, ricocheted off walls, and zinged along the concrete floor.

Bud and Joe dove behind a pile of junk just as rivets tore through it. Stuff went flying everywhere as packing crates, paint cans, and discarded boxes were riddled in the barrage.

Just as Himes ran out of ammo, Cal stalked from his office and corralled him from behind. His massive arms squeezed the runt in a bear hug until his gun clattered to the floor. Then, he shoved Himes in the bathroom and locked him in.

"That was a riveting experience," I muttered, crawling from inside my locker.

"Ha! Ha!" deadpanned Cal as he snatched up a phone to call security. "What made Himes snap, anyway?"

"Musta got one broom up the ass too many," Bud said.

"Like you didn't have anything to do with it."

"Who me?"

"Now, he'll be goin' from one loony bin to another," cackled Joe. "Only the new one will have padded walls."

"That's what happens when you're goosey," sniggered Bud. "The old nerves short-circuit, ya know."

"And both of you jokers are fired!" snapped Cal. "I looked the other way one night too many."

The Eight Point

In 1978, the first day of buck season was perfect. I parked my car just as dawn streaked the sky and trotted up a dirt driveway, across a rickety bridge, and toward a house built on a pine-clotted hillside. A fresh tracking snow had fallen overnight, but it was now cloudless with excellent visibility. Equally important, there was not one breath of wind to blow my scent to the deer I would soon stalk.

Just before reaching the house, I saw a mailbox with the name "Moyer" painted on it. There, I turned onto a trail that cut through an overgrown field. The field was a maze of frost-blasted goldenrod. It still wasn't time to hunt, so I scrambled along without worrying about the noise I made.

I loaded my rifle when my watch read seven o'clock. Entering a forest of hardwoods and hemlock, I struck another trail. Cautiously, I crept past a deserted powerhouse and on toward the ridgetop. Deer sign was everywhere from fresh piles of dung to hoof prints crisscrossing the snow. It wasn't uncommon to see herds of twenty bucks and does running together in these woods.

When I reached the summit, I stopped to catch my breath. I couldn't shoot accurately with a pounding pulse, so I sat against a tree until my heart rate returned to normal. Crawling to my feet, I moved stealthily along a dirt road that followed the ridge. I had scouted this area numerous times during squirrel season and knew where the deer ran and also where they hid. This valley was known as Indian Creek and was a refuge for all kinds of game.

I continued to sneak hunt until I reached a power line that cut across the road and over the hill to the right. I crept down the slope toward a windfall that I had chosen for my stand. The day before I had come here to cut shooting lanes through the brush. This was a prominent deer crossing, and I grinned broadly as I knelt behind the dead tree.

I had just gotten into position when I saw five does bolt out of the woods below and cross from left to right. They were a good two hundred yards away, closer to the creek than the ridge. The place they ran was a mixture of meadows and thick hemlock. It was even a long shot for my 30.06. No bucks were with the herd, so I sat to wait for more action.

I dug an apple from my pocket and took a big bite. It was cold and juicy and satisfying. I only ate half of it when I stopped in mid-chomp. A scant fifty yards off, a lone whitetail came slipping through the woods directly toward me. Each time it stopped, it kept its head behind a tree, so I couldn't get a good look at it. Dropping the apple in the snow, I raised my gun slowly and trained my scope on the illusive deer.

My pulse was now pounding again, for this deer acted like a buck. Sure enough, I caught a glimpse of horns as he darted into the next thicket. There, he stopped between two pines among the low-hanging branches.

I clicked my gun off safe and drew down on him. I trained the crosshairs on his stout neck, waiting for an unobstructed view of his head. He took one step and then another and one more still before his horns cleared the limbs. With a groan, I lowered my rifle and slumped dejectedly to the ground. It was a buck alright, but his spikes weren't four inches long. I sure wasn't going to kill an illegal deer and lose my hunting license. Hunting was my religion, and the woods, my chapel!

As the sun climbed in the blue sky, the deer grew more active. Hunters pushed them past me four more times, but they always crossed down by the stream. I saw a five point, too, but didn't want to wound him at long distance. If he ran off and died without me finding him, I'd feel horrible. Sure, I was a meat hunter, but sportsmanship meant just as much.

Finally, I rose and crept a hundred yards down the hill. Finding a large oak to hide behind, I again ducked low to keep moving deer from spotting me. I was immediately rewarded when a herd of ten whitetails appeared from nowhere and slunk past within easy range. These were all does, and I watched them until they disappeared into a patch of beech.

It was now noon, so I pulled out a sandwich and unwrapped the wax paper that covered it. As I munched on bread and cheese, I noticed two whitetails working their way toward me through the hemlock. They also were hungry and browsed on seedlings that jutted from the snow.

Boughs obscured both feeding animals, making it impossible to determine their gender. Just to be safe, I raised my rifle and focused my scope on the biggest deer. Suddenly, he lifted his head, only to have half the "branches" go with it. Those were his horns, and I wasted no time squeezing off a shot. I knew I hit him when his tail went down. *Where*, I didn't know, because he blasted off into the brush at a dead run.

I was up in an instant and scrambled to find his trail in the snow. When I reached the place he'd been feeding, I found hair and a splotch of blood. I cranked another round into my rifle and started after him. I didn't go fast but didn't go slow either. I kept one eye on the woods ahead and the other trained on the blood trail. What started as droplets soon became a red stream. He had run toward the creek, and I found him piled up just short of his destination.

I closed on him and then circled his body with my gun ready. After giving him a couple kicks with my boot, I saw that he wasn't going anywhere. My bullet had hit him in the heart, and adrenaline put him on the run. It took him a while to realize he was dead. It was when his lungs gave out and his legs folded beneath him that he finally collapsed.

Kneeling in the snow, I said a short prayer thanking God for bringing me this fine eight point. I had read that the Indians always said this prayer, and it seemed like a fine tradition to me. Killing a deer was a holy, cleansing experience, and I paid proper homage to the spirit I had extinguished.

Rolling the buck over on his back, I drew my hunting knife and slit open his belly. I had just plunged my hands into the chest cavity to withdraw the liver when a furious woman came tramping toward me. She was short and wiry and had a mop of red hair sticking out from beneath her hunting cap. Fire shot from her eyes, and her movements were brusque and exaggerated.

"You F---er!" she raged. "You stole my F---in' deer!"

It was the first time I'd heard a woman use the F word, and it kinda took my head. She was now pointing her rifle at me, and I gulped before sputtering, "What do you mean, ma'am? I shot this big fella fair an' square. I'm sure if you dig the slug outta him, you'll find it matches my .06."

"You F---er!" she wailed again. "I've been watchin' that buck the whole small game season and knew his every move. I built a tree stand above where he humped his does. I knew him that well, I did. Then, you come along. . .and stole 'im!"

"No, I *shot* him," I said evenly. "Through thick brush that coulda blowed up my bullet before it got to him."

"But he come runnin' right at me," blared the woman. "I just started squeezin' the trigger...and he fell down. Just like that! Then, I come here to find you guttin' 'im out. You F---er!"

Her last obscenity got me kinda riled. I wouldn't take such guff from a man, let alone some sassy broad. Finally, I growled, "Lady, I don't see your name on this land. Why don't you just mosey along?"

The woman's eyes narrowed into dangerous slits, and I could tell she was ready to rip into me again. It was then that I stood and drew myself up to my full height. When she saw me towering over her, I heard her choke. Then, she spotted my outstretched hand and the bloody knife I clutched in it.

After backing carefully away, the huntress stalked off. She muttered more curses as she stomped up the valley. Each oath was viler than the one it followed. Finally, she wailed just before disappearing, "My name is Wanda Moyer, you F---er! You'll pay for crossin' me!"

When I think back on it, I shoulda held my peace. Or given that crazy witch the eight point. When I went to that valley the next fall, I found all of it posted. Damn! She did own the land, and I never got to hunt there again...

Misdeeds & Misadventures

The Speedboat

Will guided his rowboat into the bay. It was made of aluminum and had a five-horse Johnson motor mounted on the back. The lad was proud to steer such a "prestigious" craft. It was four more years before he could drive a car, so captaining this vessel made him feel grown-up and independent. He wore a white sailing cap that his mom bought him in Alexandria Bay. He tipped it at his buddy, Kully, as his face spread into a wide grin.

"Take us into them lily pads," suggested Kully, pointing toward the shoreline. "There should be some bullfrogs there."

"But we didn't bring our .22's," protested Will.

"We got our fishin' poles, don't we?"

"What good'll they do?"

"Haven't you heard of catchin' frogs?"

"No. . ."

"All ya need is red cloth stuck on a hook to dangle in front of their mouths. I got some right here in my tackle box."

"Okay, but we'll have to be real quiet. Or we'll spook 'em."

Will cut the engine, and the boat glided toward shore. When it stopped short, he picked up an oar and poked it in the lake bottom to propel the craft forward. Kully, meanwhile, stood in the bow with his pole ready. As they coasted along, the boys could hear the baritone "grump" of the frogs just ahead.

"Sounds like they're sayin' *jug-a-rum*," snickered Will. "Jug of rum. Jug of rum."

"I wish we had some to drink," chuckled Kully. "It'd sure beat Croaka Cola."

As the boat slipped through the lily pads, the whine of mosquitos and the squawk of blackbirds joined the chorus of frogs. Kully motioned for Will to stop poling and carefully peered among the white and yellow flowers floating on the water. Finally, he spotted a triangular, green head protruding from the lake. Its pop-eyes housed almond-shaped pupils that protruded from the top of its skull.

Kully swung his red-clothed hook in front of the frog's mouth. Its tongue shot out, and the lad was fast to a pound of thrashing fury. The frog kicked and squirmed and bent the boy's rod as he horsed it into the boat.

"What a beauty!" yelped Kully. "Can't wait to fry his legs in butter."

"Nothin' tastier," enthused Will. "Now, let me try catchin' one."

The boys changed roles, with Kully pushing the boat and Will "fishing" from the bow. More frogs bellowed from a nearby bank, so Kully propelled them in that direction. Will saw a big male sitting on the muddy shore. It was mainly brown and blended in with its place of ambush.

Will tried three times before he dangled the hook close enough for the frog to attack it. He reefed back on the pole and yanked the bullfrog in the air. When he brought it into the boat, he gasped when he saw what the frog had for its last meal. A rattail hung from the amphibian's powerful jaws, and slime and blood dripped from it.

"What the crap," croaked Will. "M-m-maybe I should chuck this boy back."

"Don't be a sissy," razzed Kully. "You ain't gonna gut this frog. You're only gonna eat its legs."

"Okay, but let's go fishin' for bass now. I hear they're bitin' real good across the lake."

"Alright. Anything to keep you from whinin'."

Will returned to the back of the boat. Kully sat in the middle seat, placed the oars in their locks, and rowed until they had cleared the shallows. Will then gave the starting rope six vigorous tugs before the motor sputtered and burst into life. With sweat streaming down his face, the lad again grinned at his pal as they bounced across the wave-tossed water.

When the boat reached the far side of the lake, Will cut the motor, and they drifted along a rocky shore with a steep drop-off.

"This don't look bassy to me," chirped Kully. "Are you sure this is where we should fish?"

"At least the water's calm here. Let's try minnows and find out. If we're lucky, we'll catch pike, too."

The boys attached bobbers to their lines. After hooking big shiners through the back, they tossed them overboard and lounged lazily in the bottom of the boat. As the boys teased each other and watched their bobbers, the sun played tag with the clouds.

They had just gotten comfortable when a speedboat roared around a distant island and came straight at them. The craft had a wooden hull topped by a glistening windshield. Four teenagers whooped and howled as they bombed nearer.

The driver still had the throttle on full when they passed within twenty yards of Will and Kully.

Luckily, the speedboat cut across the smaller craft's bow, or its wake would have swamped the rowboat. Will shook his fist at the hooting teens only to watch them circle back and buzz even closer.

"Look! They're chuggin' beers," sang Will.

"They must be drunk. Or just plain stupid!"

As the sleek vessel bore down on them again, Kully saw a Playboy flag flying from the stern. He bellowed for the driver to peel off, but instead he flew by broadside. The resulting waves plunged the rowboat from gunwale to gunwale into the pitching lake, half filling it with water. Kully and Will were bailing like mad when the speeders returned for a third pass.

Will was beyond angry. With a growl, he fished a cannonball sinker from his soaked tackle box. He was a husky boy and could fire a baseball from home to second better than any catcher in Little League. When the speedboat closed to that same distance, Will whipped the sinker with all his might. It hit in the exact center of the windshield, and there was the smash of glass followed by a surprised curse. Immediately, the boat veered away. The last thing Will saw was the bunny flag flapping like mad behind the retreating craft.

"Who were those idiots?" cried Kully, as he returned to his bailing.

"Rich kids from the north end of the lake."

"We're lucky they didn't sink our boat."
"Yeah, we'd have lost all our fishin' gear."
"Or drown! I think we should go back to camp now."
"But we ain't caught any bass," Will moaned. "Dad'll ground me if I don't bring some home for supper. I won't be allowed to use the boat again."
"I say we go back!"
"Who's the sissy now?"
"Hey, don't call me that! I'm hot and want to go swimmin'."
"An' sniff after the babe who wears that tiger skin bikini."
"Can't help it. When she struts down the beach, I get hornier than a three-peckered goat."
"And about as talkative, too. Heck, you ain't said more 'n two words to her since she arrived Sunday."
"You don't have to talk to do what I have in mind."
"So that's why your mom washed your sheets three times this week?"
"Ha! Ha!"
After the boys finished bailing their boat, Will reluctantly started the motor. The lake was a lot choppier now, and it took them almost an hour to get home. When they finally reached the dock in front of their cottages, Kully clambered out with his tackle box and fishing rod. Will then put the boat in reverse and putted away.
"Where you goin'?" yelled Kully.
"Fishin'!"
"At least toss me them frogs before you go."

"See ya!"

Will shifted the motor to "fast" and headed toward the north. The wind picked up and pushed him briskly along. Black clouds boiled in the sky, but he *had* to catch fish for dinner. Nothing was going to deter him!

Will steered into a wave-tossed channel between shore and a crescent-shaped isle. Swinging behind the isle, he slowed his engine and entered a calm bay. Island trees blocked the wind and made it a perfect haven. The water was like glass, so Will attached a Jitterbug to his line for some surface action. The lure he chose had a yellow belly and black spots on it white sides.

Will flipped the Jitterbug near a patch of lily pads and let it float completely still. After a minute, he gave it a twitch and watched the water explode around it. He yanked back on his rod to set the hook. A smallmouth bass stood on its tail and "walked" a yard before splashing back into the bay. The fish ran and tugged and repeated its acrobatics before coming exhausted to the boat.

The incoming storm had the fish all stirred up. Will got so absorbed in catching one bass after another that he didn't notice the danger until the first raindrops fell. The sky had now turned green, and he knew it was time to beat it back up the lake. With nervous sweat popping from his brow, it took him ten full pulls of the starting rope before his five-horse burst into life.

When Will returned to the channel, he found it choked with whitecaps. He pointed his bow into them but made little headway fighting the gale-force wind. He was now heading into that wind that plucked off his sailor's cap and whisked it into the air.

"Damn!" he wailed as his cap flew away. "Mom is gonna kill me!"

The rowboat crashed through the waves, drenching Will with spray. Water now sloshed in the bottom, too, along with his bailing can. It clanked back and forth from side to side as the craft bucked and rocked. The boy was soon forced to bail with one hand and steer his boat with the other.

Will had only gotten halfway up the channel when his motor sputtered and died. Feverishly, he tugged on the starter rope but to no avail. The Johnson was flooded or out of gas. He tried to service it until his boat turned sideways, and water poured in around his ankles.

Manning the oars, Will turned his craft directly into the waves to keep it from capsizing. With fear glittering in his eyes, he reefed on them with such force that the right oar splintered and broke in half, hurling him backward. He slammed his face into the stern seat and then scrambled to retrieve the one good oar before it washed overboard. Now, he wished he'd worn a life preserver like his mother always pestered him to do.

Blood streamed from Will's nose as he perched in the bow to keep it faced into the crashing whitecaps. He paddled with the oar and glanced furtively behind him. He was being swept toward "the rocks," the worst hazard on the lake. Dad had brought him here on their first day of vacation to warn him of their menace. They jutted up from the waves to just under the surface and had wrecked more than one careless boatman. A red flag protruded from the top of them and flapped wildly in the wind. As the flag got nearer, Will discovered he was crying.

When all seemed lost, the boy heard the chug of a boat motor. Faint at first, it came directly toward him. The sound was steady and reassuring, and Will wiped the tears from his eyes. Had Kully and his pa come to save him? Or was it the conservation guys?

Will stared expectantly at the dot that appeared atop the swells. It grew into a blur and then a speeding vessel. The lad shouted into the spray and waved his arms wildly. "Here I am! Here I am!" he howled.

Will somehow kept his boat righted with the oar. His arms grew sorer by the minute as the storm worsened and the billows became more violent. He battled and prayed and hoped that his rescuers arrived...in time.

The oncoming craft was bigger than Kully's dad's but smaller than the state boy's cruiser. Will watched it bounce across the water and cheered its steady progress. He waved his oar then paddled, waved his oar then paddled. Waved—

Strangely, the boat roared faster, the closer it came. Its hull was made of wood, and a windshield kept spray from drenching the driver. That would have been true had a hole not been punched through the glass near his sneering face. Will now knew who was coming. With a gasp, he shut his eyes tight.

The River

Jimmy squirmed uneasily in the backseat of his aunt's car. He was looking out the window at the passing river, hoping the reek of her hairspray didn't make him sick. He had rolled down his window twice, but each time he was forced to roll it back up when Mrs. Morgan glared at him from the passenger seat. How his cousin, Jack, stood the stench was still a mystery. But Jack loved fishing so much, he'd walk barefoot across fields fertilized with horseshit to reach his favorite stream.

Jack's voice rang out like a pistol shot, "Stop here!" he barked. "This is where we want to fish today, Mom."

Mrs. Thompson pulled off onto the berm, and Jack and Jimmy spilled out opposite doors. The boys were dressed in shorts and sneakers and donned wide-brimmed hillbilly hats. They had identical creels strapped over their shoulders. As they leaped from the still-moving auto, they were already assembling their Zebco rods.

"Have a good time," sang Jack's mom.
"And be careful," added Mrs. Morgan.
"Yes, ma'am," replied Jimmy.
"We'll pick you after we finish shopping."

"When will that be?" asked Jack.
"Probably around three."
"See you then, Mom!"
"You bet, Son. Good luck!"

With Jack in the lead, the boys scrambled down a bank and streaked it for the river. They chattered like magpies as they crashed through head-high ferns and then through a grove of dense poplars. They pointed their rods backward to keep them from getting damaged by the brush.

When the boys reached the riverbank, they were immersed in fog rising from the gurgling water. The current was swift here but shallow enough to wade. They splashed to the other side and moved downstream toward a deep, slow-moving pool. Jack tied a minnow-style lure on the end of his line while Jimmy hooked on a night crawler. Casting into the current, they presented their offerings to the waiting fish below. Jack was soon fast to a feisty bass as his cousin tussled with a carp.

Jack landed the bass, broke its neck, and shoved it in his creel. Then, he sat on a sandbar to heckle Jimmy. His fish was far from cooperative and made one run after another up and down the pool. Jimmy was exhausted by the time he dragged the fat carp up on the beach.

"Look at the lips on that mother," teased Jack. "They remind me of the date you had last Friday."

"And who fixed me up with that skag?" fumed Jimmy.

"Hey, no one twisted your arm..."

"No, but you did tell me I couldn't come today if I didn't take out your girlfriend's pal."

"Details. Details."

Jack issued a horselaugh at his cousin's expense and tramped along the riverbank until he came to a swift run. His cast went awry, and his lure got stuck in a tree overhanging these rapids. He yanked on his monofilament line, stretching it to its limit. When he'd given up hope of rescuing his plug, it shot back at him like a bullet.

Jimmy had just released the carp into the water when he heard Jack cry, "Help! Help!" By the tone of his cousin's voice, he knew something bad had happened.

Jimmy found Jack standing in the river. A horrified look was etched on his face, and blood drizzled down his forehead. His hat had been knocked off his head, and he yanked at a glistening object stuck in his scalp. It was his lure, and both treble hooks were buried deep.

"You got yourself in a puppy snatch this time, Cuz."

"You don't have to remind me, Cuz. Just rip those dang hooks out!"

"But they're in past the barbs," protested Jimmy. "It'd be less painful if I snipped them off."

"Snip 'em? My ass! You can't ruin my last Mirro-Lure!"

"Okay, but it's gonna hurt. . ."

Jack clenched his teeth and snapped his eyes shut as Jimmy twisted and tore the plug from his scalp. Blood gushed from the wound, and his head felt like it was on fire. When the hooks were finally free, he grunted, "I'd better file them a little sharper in case I tie into a big bass."

"They're plenty sharp enough," mumbled Jimmy. "They just snagged the biggest sucker in the river."

"Ha. Ha. Carp Man. If you weren't makin' out with Missus Carp, you'd have helped me a lot sooner."

"Ah, you're just jealous you didn't catch her!"

"I stick with game fish," bragged Jack. "That's why I don't use crawlers like you."

Jack knelt at the riverside and dipped his head in the cold water to numb his pain. Then, he rose, slapped on his dripping hat, and returned to fishing.

Jimmy watched his cousin with a hurt look on his face. As he dug a red and white spoon from his creel, he murmured, "I can catch game fish, too. Who does Jack think he is, Gadabout Gaddis?"

The boys came to a stretch of stream where they'd caught some monster fish on their last trip. Despite the mist playing on the water, Jack made one pinpoint cast after another near rocks where the smallmouths lurked. He missed two strikes before tying into a huge bass. This fish knew all the tricks. After using the current to cancel the pull of Jack's rod, it stood on its tail and shook loose the lure.

"Cock-a-doodle-damn!" raged Jack, his face flushing with anger. "Knew I shoulda sharpened those hooks!"

The sun had just broken over the horizon like a fiery orb. When Jimmy saw the redness of Jack's cheeks, he said, "Need some Coppertone, Cuz? Don't want to get baked, do ya?"

"You can shove that sun screen up your rear! If its scent gets on my plug, not a fish in this river will bite it."

"Hey, bite this!" growled Jimmy, grabbing his crotch. "You don't have to take it out on me because you lost that bass."

"Yes, I do!"

The sun grew hotter by the minute, and the boys took refuge under a tall hemlock growing on the bank. While Jimmy wolfed down a baloney sandwich, his cousin popped open a Coke. He guzzled half of it in one swallow and then chugged the rest.

Leaping to his feet, Jack bellowed, "My batteries are re-charged. Let's go!"

"But can't I at least finish my lunch?"

"You can eat when we get home!"

Jimmy switched from a spoon to a Rapala to a deep-diving Vamp Spook and still had no luck. Jack, though, stuck with the Mirro-Lure and caught two legal bass. As he hauled the second one onto the shore, he cackled, "Outfought ya now, didn't I? I'm the cock of this walk, and don't you forget it!"

Jack's face and neck were Indian red, and his hands and arms even redder. His eyes blazed with another kind of fire, kindled by his competitive nature. When Jimmy suggested that they sit in the shade, his cousin spat, "Won't find fish there! I still need three for my limit."

"If you don't get sunstroke first."

"Crap-a-doodle-do! Now, you sound like Mrs. Morgan!"

The sun, though, had put the fish down, and the cousins spent two fruitless hours casting and retrieving their lures. By the time Jimmy looked at his pocket watch, it was already two-thirty. Holding it up for Jack to see, he said, "We better find a place to cross the river. We don't want to keep your mother waiting."

"Are you sure it's that late already?"

"What, are you blind?"

Only after Jimmy shoved his timepiece in his cousin's face, did Jack grudgingly stop fishing. They had come to a swift shoot of rapids that was waist-deep to the shorter boy. Jack followed the taller Jimmy, holding onto his belt for better balance. The water boiled around them and sucked at their legs as they fought against the flux.

They had only waded halfway across when Jack spied a bassy-looking pocket just downstream. Letting go of his cousin, he cast into it. His lure took a mighty jolt that jerked Jack off his feet. As he fell into the rapids with a splash, he somehow pushed the button on his reel. Then, he was swept off by the current that smashed him against rocks and dragged him repeatedly to the river bottom.

Jimmy, meanwhile, fought his way to the bank and raced downstream to track his cousin's struggles. He grabbed a stout branch that had washed up on a beach and then tore along even faster. Watching Jack's head like a bobber, he saw him enter a channel next to shore. He held out the branch as Jack swooshed by, but his cousin missed it with his free hand.

Jimmy turned and broke into a dead run. When he was twenty yards ahead of his flailing friend, he knelt at the river's edge and extended the branch over the raging torrent. This time Jack grabbed it, and Jimmy wrestled him onto the bank.

Jack gurgled and groaned and hugged the land. Then, he sat up, turned the handle on his reel, and tightened the line. He was greeted by an answering tug and found himself fast to the fish he had hooked upriver.

With water streaming from his clothes, Jack stood and fought the bass across the current. By the way it thrashed, he could tell it was a monster. He pumped his rod until he worked the fish into the shallows. When it was finally spent, he thrust his fingers into its gills and lifted it with a triumphant cry.

"You're so lucky, you could fall through an outhouse floor and come out with a lunker," teased Jimmy.

"But at least I don't kiss carp like you!"

"No, but I swear you have a dorsal fin runnin' down your back."

"And it kept me afloat 'til ya saved me, ya big lummox!"

The boys exchanged a rough hug and then tramped wearily toward the road. Jimmy turned to watch his cousin stomp along, wondering at what he saw. Jack was hatless and had a big hole ripped in his scalp. He was half-drown and thoroughly baked. His soaked sneakers squished with every step, and his drenched shirt clung to him like green skin. Weighed down by his bulging creel, he looked ready to collapse.

Jack's exhaustion, though, was the furthest thing from his mind. "Just think how many fish we'll catch once we can drive here on our own," he enthused, flashing a wide grin.

"You mean, if the river don't get us first."

"Hey, enough of that talk. There's Mom now. Can't wait to tell her about our day!"

The "Friendly" Coon

"Looks like we're here!" exclaimed Dale when he saw water shimmering just ahead through the trees.

"It's about time," moaned Mark. "Eight hours in a car ain't my idea of fun."

"But think about all the beautiful country we've seen," jabbered Chip. "The Adirondacks are awesome!"

Dale parked his car next to a camping area that stretched through the woods to the lakeshore. Each campsite came with a stone fireplace and a picnic table. The guys nestled under some pine trees that would protect them from bad weather. They set up their tent, spread their bedrolls inside, and placed their ice chest on the table. Then, they pulled their canoe down from the car roof and set their fish gear in it. Without further ado, they pushed off into the cold, clear water and headed across the lake.

While Chip and Mark paddled, Dale attached a spinner blade onto his line. A foot below it, he tied on a hook threaded with a night crawler. He trolled his bait behind the canoe, watching sunlight glint off the silver blade. As they rounded a point, his line jerked, and he was fast to a lively trout. The trout darted left then right and then left again. It shook its head furiously and splashed on the surface as it neared the canoe. Mark slipped a net under it and lifted it out of the water. Then, Mark manned the pole while Dale helped with the rowing. The guys took turns catching fish until they had enough for supper.

The fishermen beached their craft and turned it over bottom-side up. Afterward, they knelt on the shore to clean their trout.

"Look at how pink this beauty is inside," Chip said, admiring a big rainbow. "And its flesh is really firm!"

"Yeah!" exclaimed Mark. "It'll be like eating salmon."

Dale, meanwhile, collected all the fish guts and handed them to Mark. "Hey, get rid of these for us, will ya?" he asked.

"Why do I get stuck with the dirty work?"

"'Cause you've got the dirtiest hands. And make sure you toss those guts in the woods away from camp. We don't want to attract critters."

Mark, though, was too tired to listen to good advice. Exhausted from their long trip, he threw the innards into a nearby garbage can when his friends weren't looking.

The trout fried up crispy and brown in Dale's iron skillet, and he cooked potatoes and onions with them. After pounding down a couple of

Budweisers, the fishermen went immediately to sleep, full and satisfied.

The next morning, Dale was the first to crawl out of the tent. He found their garbage can tipped over and the remains of their meal strewn everywhere on the ground. When he saw fresh coon tracks in the soft sand, he bellowed, "Chip. Mark. Get out here!"

"What's wrong?" asked Mark, issuing a long yawn.

"Look at that mess! Did you dispose of those fish guts like I asked you or toss them in that can?"

"Um, I guess I messed up. . ."

"Yes, you did! Now, we'll have to burn all our table scraps to keep that coon from bugging us."

"Let's have breakfast and discuss this later," Chip said. "We've got a lot of fish to catch today and some exploring to do, too."

"Yeah, lighten up," grumbled Mark. "We're supposed to be on vacation, ya know."

The guys didn't return to camp until sundown. Along with six trout, they brought back a bucket of crayfish. After being in the blazing sun all day, it didn't take many beers to get them ossified. Their trout dinner was as good as the night before, but the boiled crayfish were overdone. In a drunken fury, Chip chucked the whole pot on the ground and then passed out in the tent.

The sun had risen well in the sky before the guys stirred in their sleeping bags. Around nine a.m.,

Mark cracked a loud fart and said, "There's the alarm clock, boys. I guess it's time to get up."

"You stinkin' hog!" yelped Dale, boiling out of his bedroll. "That's what I call a crime against nature!"

Chip, meanwhile, scrambled outside for some fresh air only to find their campsite again in shambles. "Frickin' coon!" he roared. "The SOB came back again!"

After breakfast, the cursing fishermen policed their campsite, dumped all the refuse and crayfish remains in the garbage can, and put a heavy rock on the lid to secure it. Then, they piled into Dale's car to go stream fishing. Chip saw the Marble River marked on the topo map and thought it looked like a good spot. Dale followed his directions until they arrived at the swift Adirondack treasure.

The fishermen cast everything they had into the rapids and pools. They tried worms, spoons, Joe's Flies, and Muddler Minnows. Although they could see big brown trout cruising around in the water, the fish refused to bite.

Finally, they came to narrow feeder stream running through a field. It looked more like a ditch than a creek. In desperation, Dale crept up it and cast a worm into the first hole he spied. His bait no sooner hit the water when a black shape darted out from under a bank and nailed it. After much tugging and pulling, Dale yanked a nine inch brookie out of the water.

"Well, I'll be dipped!" he yelled. "I finally found a hungry trout."

Mark stole along the bank until he saw where the water cut in beneath it. Flipping a worm upstream, he let it roll naturally along with the current until it was viciously attacked. There was no place to maneuver this fish, so he horsed it onto the meadow. His trout was another keeper.

The guys worked their way up the creek, catching fish in quick succession. They returned to the car with bulging vests and wide grins. They yakked all the way back to their campsite about their wonderful luck and arrived just after dark. As their headlights fell across their tent, they saw a mammoth coon prowling nearby. It had been in their garbage again, and Dale cursed when he saw the mess it had made.

"Let's tree that SOB!" yelped Chip, leaping from the car.

"I'm with you!" shouted Mark. "Git 'im!"

As the angry men chased the coon up a nearby pine, Dale fetched a pump-up pellet pistol from beneath the driver's seat. Joining his friends, he loaded it and said, "Look what I brought along for an emergency."

"Beats throwing rocks at that bugger," growled Chip, "even if it is illegal here."

Dale pumped the gun to the maximum and fired it at the treed coon. He heard a loud thud as the pellet hit the carnivore in the back. Mark had retrieved a flashlight from the glove compartment and shined it on their target. The coon snarled when caught in the light and wrapped its ringed tail tighter around its body.

Dale peppered the coon until blood ran down the trunk below it. He shot twenty pellets into the beast, and still it clung to the tree. "How tough is that critter, anyhow?" he wondered aloud. "Damn! I'm out of ammo."

"Now, what are we going to do?" cried Chip. "We can't just leave him there to suffer."

"How can we finish him off? He's up too high to hit with a rock. And I'm not gonna climb up there after him."

"You, of all people, know how vicious a cornered coon is," jabbered Mark, "after watching one kill your grandpa's best hound."

"Yeah. . .I remember."

"Then, I guess we should leave him there to die."

"Don't have much choice. Next time, I'll bring more pellets."

The guys returned to their campsite to cook their day's catch. They were out of beer and ate the food without tasting it. Nervously, they retired to their tent to play cards. Before starting a round of poker, Chip lit the camp lantern. He placed it in the mouth of the tent as if to ward off evil.

A brisk wind rustled the branches above them and foretold the arrival of an electric storm. Another storm arrived first clad in bleeding flesh. As Dale shuffled the cards, a hellish snarl entered their shelter and bounced around the canvas. The deck spilled from his hands when he turned to face the wounded coon. All he could see were its glittering eyes and bared, gnashing fangs.

While Dale sat frozen in horror, Mark scrambled into action. Yanking his filet knife from a sheath on his belt, he sliced a jagged hole in the back of the tent and ran to lock himself in the car. Only Chip remained cool. Snatching up their spare paddle, he bashed at the coon until it retreated into the darkness.

Wailing in agony, the coon attacked the garbage can, the ice chest, and whatever else it encountered. It issued one hair-raising scream after another as it ripped and tore and smashed and crashed until its fury was lost in a loud peal of thunder. Then, the thunder conquered all.

The storm raged until the wee hours of the morning as Chip and Dale huddled fearfully together. Rain fell in sheets, and wind rocked the tent until the guys thought it would blow into the lake. The lightning was so frequent, they dared not venture outside.

When things got calm at daybreak, they heard the car door open. Emerging from the tent flaps, they saw Mark scurrying toward them.

"W-w-why didn't you come join me?" he stammered. "To be s-s-safe."

"That'll only happen if we move to a different campground," muttered Dale, surveying the wreckage around him.

"Yeah, look at what that coon did!" exclaimed Chip.

The garbage can was bent and battered, and their ice chest lay lidless in a puddle of mud. The food that been stored inside was strewn everywhere. Even their clothes had been mauled. The rain slickers that had hung outside were chewed and clawed apart. The same with their sneakers.

"C-c-come on. Let's go!" urged Mark.

"Without having breakfast first?"

"There's nothing left to eat," Chip said, pointing to broken eggshells and a loaf of soggy bread.

"Then, let's get the flock outta here!" yelped Mark. "We can eat down at the trading post."

"Are you buying?" asked Dale.

"You bet! Now, get off your dead ass and help me lift this canoe."

Kinzua Beach

The first real job I had was with the U.S. Forest Service at Kinzua Beach. I was part of the crew that mowed lawns, cleaned restrooms, and policed the grounds. I had just graduated from high school and worked with two other recent grads, Bob and Lenny. Bob was a real strong dude with bulging biceps who was there to get a tan. Lenny had long, dark hair and a darker sense of humor. He would have laughed had a lightning storm killed everyone on the beach.

The first thing we learned is that people are pigs! We had only been there a couple of days when the water pump broke, forcing us to close the bathrooms. We couldn't shut the bathhouse, though, because bathers needed a place to change their clothes. To keep them from using the toilets, we hung up "Out of Order" signs. As an added precaution, we crawled under the stall doors and locked them from the inside.

Of course, that didn't deter the public. We came back the next morning to find every john full to the seat with crap. The stench was sickening as we scooped shit into buckets and disposed of it in garbage cans outside. Bob and I took turns throwing up. We cursed the perpetrators and their kids and grandkids. Lenny only wondered how many asses squatted there to make this mess.

"Why didn't you get the shit truck to suck out these toilets?" I asked the boss. "That's how they drain the outhouses at Jake's Rocks."

"Because this will build character in you boys," he replied with a sneer.

"And I'd like to stuff you in headfirst," mumbled Bob, so that I only heard.

"What did you say?"

"I was just agreeing with you, sir."

Another day I was cleaning the ladies' room. I entered a real smelly stall and closed the door behind me. Even after I had poured bleach in the toilet and swirled it around with a brush, the stink remained. I learned why when I turned to leave. There, dangling from the coat hook on the back of the door, was a bloody Kotex just inches from my nose. I sure threw up a lot that first week!

To have the courage to go back on Friday, I got drunk the night before. I arrived at the ranger station still pretty lit. My head started swirling as soon as I got in the truck that took us to Kinzua Beach. We had only driven a short ways when I started to retch. As my stomach churned and gurgled, I yelled for the boss to stop. Lee was his name, and he only complied to keep from smelling my vomit. He cursed me the whole time I puked along the road.

To punish me further, Lee gave me every dirty job he could think of. I was back in the nasty ladies' room in the morning while he stayed to "supervise." Then, he pulled on a white glove to see if I'd missed any dirt. When he found one small speck above the mirror, he peeled me up one side and down the other.

"Now, go mow the hill by the beach," he snarled. "That'll sweat the beer out of you!"

Yeah, the boss was a real pain in the jar. He was studying to be a surgeon and already thought he was Dr. frickin' Kildare. Man, he cut us no slack at all. He got on Lenny about the length of his hair and called him a "hippie fag." Then, he screamed at Bob when he caught him with his shirt off 'til I thought he'd break a blood vessel.

"I'll fire you the next time," Lee yelled, "for breaking federal regs! We must look presentable to the public. At all times! Do you hear? Without exception!"

"Screw the public," muttered Bob under his breath. "They're the ones that bury us in shit."

"What'd you say?"

"Anything to please the public, sir."

The next day Bob wore a jacket to work. When he took it off, the boss about threw a shit fit! Underneath, Bob had on a muscle shirt with the sleeves cut off to the armpits. Because his back and chest were covered, there wasn't anything Lee could do but fume.

Another time I was told to pick up trash that was strewn in the bushes near the picnic area. I had just entered the tall grass when a snake slithered between my feet and crawled toward the garbage. The snake was at least four feet long and had a triangular head.

With a squawk, I turned and raced back to the lawn. I was greeted by the furious Lee, who immediately got in my face and yelled, "You're disobeying a direct order, fella! Get your ass back there and collect that trash."

"Rattler!" I cried. "Almost stepped on it!"

"A likely story! The only rattlers around here are up in the rocks. What? Do you want me to hold your hand?"

"No, but you can go see for yourself. . ."

The boss puffed out his chest and struck boldly off into the brush. He had only taken a few steps when a warning rattle froze him in his tracks. Backing carefully away, he returned white-faced to my side.

"You can leave that trash for later," Lee croaked. "Come on! I have a different job for you."

"And I'll bet it's worse than this one," I lamented.

Another scary incident happened late one afternoon. Lenny and I were policing the area near the ladies' room when we found a young coon trapped in a garbage can. He had somehow leaped inside to feast on trash and had eaten so much he couldn't get out. When we came upon him, he was totally pissed. He frothed and snarled and bared his teeth until we backed off to consider our options.

"What do you think?" I asked, pulling nervously at my short-sleeved shirt.

"All that critter wants is let loose. Let's dump the can, so he can escape."

"But what if he attacks us? You saw how mad he is."

"I know a girl lives on a hill," cackled Lenny. "She won't do it, but her sister will!"

While reciting his goofy poem, Lenny made a mad dash for the garbage can. He knocked it over with a clatter. The coon spilled out and streaked for the ladies' room. The door was propped open, and he scrambled in where it was dark. Screams immediately pierced the air as a troop of Girl Scouts came rushing outside, many still pulling up their pants.

Lenny and I laughed until tears streamed down our faces. That was until Lee showed up on the scene.

"What's going on here?" he yelled.

"A coon just ran into the restroom," snorted Lenny.

"Well, go catch it!"

"With what?" I asked. "It sure won't be my hands!"

"Or mine, either," said Lenny. "You better call the rangers for this job."

"Are you disobeying a direct order?"

"No," we sang in unison. "We're just being smarter than you!"

"Then, I'll go grab it and release it into the woods."

"I hope you've had your rabies shots," warned Lenny, snarling like a cornered coon.

"Um. . .maybe I will call the rangers."

Lee continued to ride our butts the whole month of June. On the morning after July 4th, he looked a little sick while he drove us to Kinzua Beach. When he burped, we caught the scent of schnapps and noticed how glassy his eyes were. He was also more miserable than usual and about bit our heads off when we asked if he was okay.

As soon as we arrived at the picnic area, the boss dug three shovels out from behind the backseat of the truck. Handing them to us, he snapped, "I want you boys to dig a ditch from here down to the lake. This ground is soggy and needs drained."

"But that will take all day," groused Lenny.

"Just shut up and do it! It will make men of you."

"Can we at least have work gloves?" I inquired politely.

"Gloves are for pussies," barked Lee. "I'll pick you up at quittin' time."

Lee drove the truck down the driveway and parked it in front of the bathhouse. Getting groggily to his feet, he made his rounds and then disappeared into the lawnmower shed. When he didn't come out with any equipment, Bob growled, "Why, that SOB has gone to sleep it off!"

"Or so he thinks," chortled Lenny, flashing a devious grin.

"What do ya have in mind?" I mumbled.

"We should nail Lee's nuts to a stump and push him off backwards," Bob yelped.

"No, my idea is better."

"Okay. Whatever it is, I'm in. We've taken more 'n our share of crap from that asshole!"

After Lenny told us his plan, we sneaked snickering across the picnic area and the lawn beyond. Holding his finger to his mouth to silence us, Lenny crept up to the shed, slipped his shovel through the twin door handles, and effectively trapped Lee inside.

Snatching the shovel from my hand, Lenny began pummeling the tin sides of the shed until it clanged deafeningly with each blow. When Lee cried, "What the hell?" Bob joined in and bashed away until his palms blistered. Then, he handed me his shovel, so I could get in my licks.

At first, Lee shouted in a commanding voice, "I know who's out there. Stop at once, or I'll fire your asses! You hear me? I'll fire you!"

None of us were dumb enough to answer. We kept hammering away while the boss tried desperately to open the door. When he couldn't get out no matter how hard he pushed, his defiance turned to pleading. Then, he began to whimper like a dog. We kept it up for a half hour straight until sobs leaked from inside the shed. At that point, Lenny pulled his shovel from the door handles, and we ran like hell.

By the time the boss crawled outside, we were already back to work. After ralphing five or six times, he wiped his mouth on his shirt sleeve and strode with menace across the picnic area. Bob and I were whistling nonchalantly when he descended upon us like a rudely awakened bear.

Growling and sputtering, Lee stepped up to Lenny. Before he got out one word, Lenny said, "Gee, boss. Look at how much we got done. Our ditch is deep enough to bury a body in."

Lee glanced at Lenny then at his shovel then back at Lenny again. Lenny flashed him a wicked grin and began gouging at the earth like he loved his work. Meanwhile, he sang in his goofy, off-key voice, "I know a girl from Californy. She ain't very pretty, but she sure is horny."

Lee turned on his heels and stalked off. Because he never *saw* who had hammered the shed, he knew he couldn't fire us. What he did do was lose his white glove and surly attitude. Our jobs remained pretty shitty, but from then on it was just due to the public. . .

The Panty Raid

The semester had been a bad one for the three Mikes. As their grades began to plummet, they learned that a "sophomore slump" didn't just occur in baseball. One of the Mikes was the centerfielder, the second a starting pitcher, and the other the first baseman. They knew Coach Heap would kill them if they flunked out, so they pounded the books nonstop to prepare for their midterms.

After they had studied their brains out for two solid weeks, the first Mike slammed his book shut and yelled, "Enough is enough! I'm ready to go ape!" He was a hyper, wiry dude who never gained a pound no matter how many plates of spaghetti he ate. Because he looked like he was still in junior high, his pals called him "the Kid."

"Then, why don't we go see the flick they're showing at the caf?" suggested Mike #2. A serious guy with horn rimmed glasses, he wore a Beatle haircut and was the only one who kept the name "Mike."

"What's it about?" asked the third Mike, a heavyset power hitter who could drink his weight in beer. He went by the nickname "Jasper" that he'd been tagged with for his naughty behavior as a child.

"It's some sort of television parody. It's even shown on closed circuit TV and is supposed to be a laugh riot."

"Then, screw studying!" exclaimed the Kid. "Let's watch it!"

The guys swarmed from their dorm room and shot down the hill toward a mob of students who were pushing their way into the cafeteria. Using Jasper as a bulldozer, they plowed inside and found a single television standing in the corner of the downstairs lounge. The chairs were already filled, so they flopped on the floor and got comfortable.

When the room was packed to capacity, the TV burst into life. The program looked handmade by college students, but the lack of production didn't detract from its humor. Like Mike had heard, "The Groove Tube," as it was called, was totally off-the-wall. First, there was "The Koko Show" hosted by a clown who read porn to children after he told the "big people" to leave the room. This was followed by the "Safety Sam" public service announcement warning viewers about VD. Sam was a puppet with a scrotum head and a penis for a nose. The Mikes totally cracked up when the Brown 25 commercial extolled the virtues of a new building material produced by Uranus. A nonsensical cooking show, wacky newscasts, and other goofy segments sent the guys into one laughing jag after another.

As the Mikes exited the caf still howling with laughter, they bumped into their buddy Rick, who lived on the same dorm floor. Rick owned a car he called Bubbles. He had hand-painted her with a brush when a body shop wanted too much money to do the job the traditional way.

"Hey, why don't we head up the road?" said Rick. "I could use a cold brew, even if this is Tuesday."

"Let's go to the Green Shingles and find us some hogs!" bawled Jasper. "We'll ride 'em 'til they squeal!"

"Or, in your case, *giggle* after they see your pee-pee," heckled the Kid.

"What do ya mean? I'm hung like a horse —"

"Fly!"

"Then, I'll tickle 'em to death!" snorted Jasper with a good-natured guffaw.

The Green Shingles was just over the New York State line where the drinking age was eighteen. The Mikes didn't find any loose women there, but they did manage to run into some beers. It didn't take them long to get drunk as rats. Mike got there the quickest. After he fell down on the way to the piss house and knocked over a waitress on the way back, the whole crew got the bum's rush out the door.

As they staggered to the car, Jasper slurred, "Damn you, Mike, you hold your liquor like a pussy."

"How would you know? You ain't ever seen one!"

"Yes, he has," sniggered the Kid. "All he has to do is look between his legs."

"That's harsh!" exclaimed Jasper. "Boy, you *did* need a break from studying."

On the way back to campus, Rick broke into a rousing rendition of "Bang Bang Lulu." He had a great voice heard often in his church choir at home. The Mikes screamed out the chorus at the top of their lungs when Rick finished each of the ninety-nine verses. They were still "singing" when they turned up the drive that wound steeply uphill to the college parking lot.

The Mikes helped each other out of Rick's car and stumbled home. On the way, they heard a ruckus coming from a girls' dormitory. They found a mob of guys yelling up at coeds leaning from a second story window. The girls were flashing their tits and teasing the hell out of the crowd. Finally, they pushed their stereo speakers up to the glass and blasted Badfinger's anthem, "If You Want It Here It Is Come and Get It," down on their audience. As an added enticement, they dangled their bras out the window.

At that exact moment, an unsuspecting girl opened the locked side entrance of the dorm. She wore Coke bottle glasses and had her hair tied up in a bun. Before she could shut the door behind her, she was inundated by a flood of crazed guys yelling, "Panty raid! Panty raid!" Books and papers went flying as the girl was knocked backward. The Mikes trampled her when they flew by with the track team. Rick, though, went home, knowing trouble when it saw it.

His eyes glittering with drunken lust, Jasper screamed, "On to Seventh Heaven, boys!"

"Yeah!" howled the Kid. "Let's do it!"

The seventh floor housed Alpha Ro sorority. From their own dorm high on the hill, the Mikes had peered in on those chicks with binoculars and had seen bare asses more than once. As they sped up the stairs, they dreamed of boobs and velvety skin. Their imaginations worked faster than their legs as they burst through the top floor door.

Instead of a harem of babes in lingerie, the Mikes saw girls in bathrobes and faces plastered with goop. After gawking in disbelief, they streaked for the nearest room. They forced their way in and began yanking bras, panties, and nightgowns from the chests of drawers. Screams rattled their eardrums as girls in curlers scrambled for the hall. The same scenario repeated itself as they raided room after room until their arms cradled a huge stash of silken delights.

With whoops of victory echoing from their throats, the Mikes returned to the hall only to find their way blocked by a battle line of angry Alpha's. They were armed with brooms, rolling pins, and buckets of water. Their eyes shot fire, and their teeth gnashed in their cursing mouths.

They reminded the Kid of Amazon warrior women when they sang a defiant chant.

Jasper lowered his head and pawed the floor like a bull. As steam shot from his nose, he rumbled forward with Mike and the Kid running in his wake. The girls locked arms and dug in their heels. There was a mighty collision followed by a loud "oof." Half the girls went ass over teacups. Those still standing closed around the Mikes and pummeled them with brooms and derision. Others slashed with their nails or smashed with their fists. There were curses of joy and curses of pain as the melee swirled toward a red exit sign.

With a yelp, the Kid broke free from the Ro who clawed him. Jasper and Mike untangled themselves at the same time. As one, the bruised boys blasted through the exit door and tore off down the stairs. A chorus of "Assholes! Morons!" followed their descent as they wound ever downward. When they reached the third floor, the Kid felt something heavy swoosh by his head as a bucket full of water shot past. He heard it crash on the tile below and looked up to see an irate coed flipping him off.

The guys flew down the rest of the stairs and out the side door of the dorm. When Mike finally managed to catch his breath, he wheezed, "Man, were those girls pissed!"

"Tell me about it," muttered the white-faced Kid. "If that bucket had hit me, it'd have split my head like a watermelon."

"Yeah, you'd think we stole their virginity instead of a few pair of bloomers."

"Shit!" wailed Jasper. "There ain't a cherry left among those sluts."

"I wonder how the other guys did?" panted Mike. "The ones who weren't stupid enough to go to the top floor."

"Hey, we ain't stupid," Jasper chirped. "When it comes to the babes, we always go *all the way.*"

"At least that's what you tell your hand."

It wasn't until the Mikes were safely locked in their room that they realized they still clutched the spoils of their raid. But the buzz of their drunk was now replaced by a nagging fear, and they jumped when a sharp rap came on the door.

"W-w-who is it?" stammered Mike.

"It's Butros! Come down to the lounge. We're takin' pictures."

"Of what?"

"Just come down. You'll laugh your ass off!"

Cautiously, the Mikes creaked open their door and crept to the downstairs lounge. Inside, they saw a celebrating mob dressed in stolen women's underwear. Many of the guys portrayed sheiks with teddies wrapped around their heads for turbans. Others acted totally gay.

Guffawing like a delighted mule, Jasper pulled on a nightgown and flounced inside to join the photo session. He preened like a lingerie model as the other Mikes snapped on bras and batted their eyes at the camera. The session went on past midnight, and no one noticed the angry stares peering in on the pageantry from outside.

Battling fatigue from their recent misadventure, the Mikes were back at the library when it opened at eight a.m. They spent the day writing compositions until their bloodshot eyes ached. For lunch they munched crackers to settle their queasy guts. They finished just as the library closed, and the sun sank behind the hillside campus.

Returning to their dorm, they found the place in an uproar. The halls rang with curses as guys trooped back and forth gesturing wildly. When the Kid asked what had happened, he was told by one of the track guys, "Freakin' chicks pulled a raid on us! The bitches!"

The Mikes stormed up the stairs to see their door standing wide open. When they looked inside, they found all their belongings missing. It wasn't just their clothes and toiletries. Even their beds and dressers were gone.

After exhaling a low whistle, Mike exclaimed, "Damn it, Jasper! You were the last one out. You were supposed to lock up."

"Uh, sorry, man. Why, they even kifed my Boone's Farm wine bottle collection!"

"And my Clemente posters," moaned the Kid.

"Just be glad they didn't steal our places on the baseball team!"

"How could they do that?"

"If they'd have gotten our comps, we'd be totally screwed!"

"And that's why it pays to procrastinate," droned Jasper. "We'll keep our papers with us 'til we hand 'em to prune-faced Hindman Friday morning."

"But where will we sleep?" bitched Mike. "On the hard floor?"

"Those broads couldn'ta carried our beds too far," replied the Kid. "I'll check the study lounge. You look in the bathroom."

"That's the first good idea you've had this semester. I need to barf, so I'll take care of that, too, while I'm there."

"Once a pussy always a pussy."

"But at least I don't squat to pee like you, Jasper."

The Infestation

When Rick didn't see the three Mikes at the campus library Thursday night, he thought he'd better check on them. They had put their room back together after finding their furniture in the study lounge and obtaining more stuff from home. It was strange that they weren't cracking the books, so he was worried they had fallen into their old habits that got them into trouble so often.

Rick climbed the stairs of the dormitory to the third floor. He just started up the hall when he saw a coed sneak from the Mikes' room and disappear down a far staircase. Her hair was disheveled, and she tugged at her dress to straighten it. She stuffed her stockings in her purse just as she disappeared from view.

Rick rapped on the Mikes' door, and a leering Jasper answered it. "Oh, I thought it was Annie comin' back for more," he sniggered.

"Annie?"

"Yeah, she just pulled the train on us."

"And you could have been the caboose," blared the Kid, "if you'd have been here a minute ago. Where were you, anyhow?"

"Studying. Like you should have been to stay out of trouble with Coach Heap."

"We were havin' a heap more fun with Annie. Toot! Toot!"

"And we sure pleasured her," crowed Mike. "She walked out of here bowlegged as a sailor."

"That girl's a real snake," declared Rick. "It's a wonder she didn't crawl away on her belly. See you clowns later."

"At least stay long enough for a brew," urged Jasper, fetching a cold one from a tub of ice in his closet.

"Did I hear someone say *beer*?" sang a studious-looking dude, sticking his head in the doorway.

"Uh. . .no, Rod," lied Mike.

"I wondered why there was so much noise coming from in here. You were having a party."

"We'd never do such a thing!"

"And what was all that grunting about?"

"We were doin' cals for baseball," chortled the Kid.

"Then, what's that smell? Unless you sweat Estee Lauder when you exercise, you're feeding me a line of crap."

"Not us!"

"Sure. . . I'll be making my rounds again in a half hour. When I return, I don't want to find any Budweiser. Or chicks, either!"

"Okay, Rod, we hear you loud and clear," said Mike, slamming the door in the fuming dude's face.

"Man, you guys coulda really got busted," croaked Rick.

"Yeah, but Rod's a cool guy," said the Kid. "He worked in a foundry before gettin' the job as our R.A. He lives in the real world. Not one filled with bullshit."

"Well, he didn't say how to get rid of this brew," cackled Jasper, "so let's chug the rest. We can chuck the cans out the window before he gets back..."

Rick was already seated in English class the next morning when the Mikes came trooping in scratching their privates. They looked like they hadn't slept much, and each of them yawned in turn as they set their compositions on Mrs. Hindman's desk. The professor was tall and gaunt, and her garish attire shocked Rick awake. That day she wore a polka-dot pink jumper with orange bows tied in her hair.

After the Mikes sat down, they squirmed and fidgeted as Mrs. H said, "Get out a piece of paper, students. It's time for your pop quiz."

As usual, the Mikes hadn't read their assignment, but that wasn't the only reason for their discomfort. No matter how they tried, they couldn't stop itching. Finally, Jasper couldn't take it anymore. He was only halfway through the quiz when he boiled out of his seat and shot across the hall to the men's room. He was going to fail the test anyway.

After class, Rick said on the way back across campus, "What ails you guys today? Are you having an allergic reaction to all that beer you guzzled?"

"We don't know," replied Mike. "We just itch all over."

"Then, why do you just scratch your balls?"

"Not sure," muttered the Kid.

"'Cause that's your nerve center," needled Rick. "I've got it all figured out."

The guys tore into the caf just before the breakfast line closed. The scrambled eggs had chopped up hotdogs in them and were congealed in greasy clumps on the plate. The only thing edible were the sticky buns. As the Kid wolfed down four of them, he chirped, "Man, these kinda remind me of Annie. S-w-e-e-t!"

"Yeah!" thundered Jasper. "She's sittin' on a goldmine!"

"And she's so giving," blabbed Mike, as he resumed his scratching.

The Mikes continued to extol Annie's virtues until they returned to their dorm. Rick rolled his eyes, said goodbye to his pals, and then went to answer nature's call. As he seated himself on the john, a host of black dots swarmed onto his leg. Brushing himself wildly, Rick let out a shriek and flew from the stall.

Rod was shaving at a nearby sink. When he saw Rick swatting at his thigh, he growled, "What the hell's wrong with you?"

"Come look!" yelped Rick, pointing at the toilet seat.

"Well, I'll be damned. Those are crabs!"

"It's all the Mikes' fault! And that sleaze, Annie!"

"I'd better call the dean. He'll get the fumigators!"

After placing his call, Rod stormed off to the Mikes' room. He found them furiously scratching as they danced to "In-A-Gadda-Da-Vida" blasting from their stereo. Their beds were unmade, and their clothes strewn across the floor. All they had on was their underwear. Their fingers were dug deep into them.

"You idiots infested the whole floor with crabs!" shouted Rod above the blaring music. "You better go to the infirmary and get some shampoo."

"Why?" quipped Jasper. "Do the crabs have dirty hair?"

"No, but you're going to have a black eye if you ever bring sluts onto this floor again."

"What do you mean?"

"Rick told me all about it."

"The rat!"

"Get dressed! The fumigators will be here soon. And wash your sheets and infested clothes, you morons!"

Although Rod's harsh comments were meant for their own good, the Mikes couldn't help but laugh. After pulling on his pants, Jasper went to his desk and wrote on two sheets of paper. Showing his signs to his buddies, they stole off chuckling to the john.

Mike hung one warning on the wall: "Don't throw toothpicks in the urinals. Crabs can pole vault." Jasper, meanwhile, taped the other on the mirror. It said, "To cure the crabs, drop your shorts and bend over facing here. When the vermin jump for the other ass, run like hell!" Both notices were signed by the Pennsylvania Board of Health.

The Fish Wardens

Back in the 1970's, I was a fanatical brook trout fisherman. Being a high school teacher gave me spring weekends and all summer to tramp the wilderness streams that ran up every McKean County hollow. Undisturbed by the current plague of loggers, developers, and gear grinding ATV's, a man could really enjoy the pristine beauty of babbling water and the scrappy, little brookies that waited to strike.

My enthusiasm for fishing also spilled over into the classroom. I talked so much about my plentiful catches that soon I had all sorts of kids pestering me to take them along.

Finally, the last Saturday before summer recess, the phone rang at dawn. On the other end of the line an excited voice jabbered, "This would be just the day to hit the creek, wouldn't it, Mr. R? I got my pole rigged and my boots on..."

Even half asleep, I recognized the squeaky enthusiasm of Dick Hale, the wide-eyed freshman who sat in the front row of my second period class. He was forever reading me angling tips from *Field and Stream* or ambushing me in the hall to talk trout. He had the bug real bad!

"Pick you up in a half hour," I mumbled after checking the clock on my nightstand. "Bring a lunch. We'll be gone all day."

"All day? You bet, Mr. R!"

I hadn't tried Buck Lick that spring and figured it would be the perfect place for Dick to catch his limit of eight trout. The creek literally teemed with fat brookies and was seldom frequented by other anglers who would spook elusive fish if they went up the stream ahead of us. I wanted the lad to succeed in the worst way, considering how much brass it took him to make that dawn phone call.

Buck Lick flowed into Sugar Run in the Allegheny River Basin. All the way there Dick squirmed with anticipation and yakked and yakked about the rod-bending monsters he hoped to land that day. His curly, straw-colored hair stuck out from beneath his ball cap, and a big grin wreathed his flushed face.

I didn't want to dampen Dick's zeal, but finally the teacher came out in me when I said, "Although we should have plenty of action today, most of our catch will be barely legal. You do remember there's a size requirement for trout?"

"Uh, what do ya mean?"

"A fish must be six inches long before you can keep it. If I were you, I wouldn't take home anything under six and a half. A dead trout shrinks when it's lain in a creel for several hours."

"I didn't bring a ruler. Do you have one, Mr. R?"

"As a matter of fact, I do. And how's your bait supply?"

"I brung plenty of night walkers. Shoot! I've got enough for two days."

"All right! You know, I heard of a boy who ran out of bait and started digging along the bank for some. Not long after, he shouted to his dad, 'Look at all these bitin' worms I found.' Here, he had dug up a whole nest of baby rattlesnakes and had to be rushed to the hospital."

"Ah, Mr. R, I ain't that dumb!"

"I didn't mean you were," I replied with a sheepish grin. "I just wanted to warn you that there are rattlers where we'll be fishing today, so be on the lookout. Don't step over a log before checking what's on the other side."

"No problem, sir. Bring on them trout!"

I barely parked my Ford along Sugar Run Road when Dick exploded from the passenger seat and began assembling his eight-foot fly rod. I scrambled to pull on my waders and stick together my own pole. After slinging a creel over my shoulder, I charged off down a well-traveled path with Dick as my shadow.

We scurried along until we reached a broad stream that glinted in the early morning sunlight. When the lad stopped to cast into the first hole we saw, I shouted over the roar of the current, "This is the main creek. It's pretty fished out. Come on!"

I led the boy down a muddy trail sprinkled with slippery rocks. After skating along for fifteen minutes, we came to a brook that dumped into Sugar Run from a hemlock-choked valley. It was only half as wide as the bigger stream but was cold and swift and made the perfect habitat for hungry brookies.

I let out a whoop when I spied Buck Lick. To reach it, I forded the rapids of the main creek. Dick got a bootful while splashing across but didn't complain.

We caught one trout after another once we started up the tributary. As luck would have it, though, only the five inchers were biting that day. After we'd gone a full mile upstream, I hadn't landed one keeper. That didn't prevent me from admiring the fierce little brookies that attacked my bait. From the sunlit riffles came sleek, silvery fish while coal black beauties lived under rocks. The males had their trademark hooked jaws and bright orange fins that I always found fascinating.

The only legal trout I hooked by noon was a nine inch native brown. It bulled deep and tugged and pulled until I dragged it up on the bank. I almost hated to take its life and dull the blood red spots that peppered its sides.

Dick, meanwhile, seemed to have little trouble hauling in keepers. Every time I passed him, he was cleaning another trout. His canvas creel was bulging with limp cargo by the time we stopped to eat lunch. Dick's eyes glistened with so much excitement that I hated to harp on the size limit thing again. I had given him a ruler at the car, so I could only hope he had taken my advice on the subject.

The long afternoon shadows stretched from the hemlocks before we began our return trek back to the main stream. Dick had caught eight legal trout to my three, and the walk down a slick deer path did little to slow his good-natured needling.

"Wait 'til I tell my buddies about my catch," he kept saying. "I can't believe I outfished you, Mr. R!"

"But I got the only brownie," I reminded him.

"Hey, maybe they'll read on the school announcements that I got my first limit. How many trout did you say you caught again?"

"Three," I chuckled. "Yeah, you whipped me good. I hope that's not on the announcements, too."

By the time we reached Sugar Run, Dick had stopped chirping his victory song. We were both leg weary from our long hike across broken ground, so we cut straight up to the road for an easier walk back to the car.

We had just spotted my blue Ford when a Willies Jeep bombed around the corner and skidded to a halt within inches of our boots. My mouth flew open in disbelief as a fat-jowled fellow with squinty eyes rolled down his window and blared, "Hey, lemme see yer fish!"

Before Dick or I could answer, the man boiled out of his vehicle and shoved a glinting badge in my face. "I'm Clinton Wilber, fish warden. Lemme see your fish!"

When I didn't respond quickly enough for the warden, he drew back his olive drab jacket to reveal a bulging gut and a hog-leg pistol stuck in his belt. Irritated by his rudeness, I tossed him my creel, and he unceremoniously dumped its contents on the road. Out spilled a pack of hooks, two tubes of split shot, a tape measure, a fish knife, a sandwich wrapper, a half empty container of worms, and three dead trout. The latter he measured with my own rule, grunting disappointedly when each was legal.

While Wilber checked my catch, the blood drained out of Dick's face. He began to edge slowly toward the woods, glancing furtively at the lanky deputy who had jumped down from the rattletrap Jeep.

"Not so fast, Sonny!" barked the deputy. "Don't even think about boltin'. I ain't much to look at, but I've been knowed to run down a deer er two."

"Yeah!" growled Wilber. "Git over here, boy. Lemme see yer fish."

Dick handed over his canvas creel and cringed when the warden stuck his sausage-sized fingers inside and produced the tiniest trout. Without its innards, the brookie looked too thin to bother cooking. Fresh from the water it might have been six inches if its back was broken and it was stretched real hard. With Wilber manning the rule, the fish barely measured five and three-quarters.

The warden rubbed his bulging gut in a satisfied way and then laid the rule on the next puny fish.

"Five and seven-eighths," he chortled gleefully. "Looks like you're gonna owe us a nice chunk o' change."

Only one of Dick's trout was legal. Wilber even took it when he rounded up the rest of the boy's catch. "See you in court, Sonny," he growled, after grilling Dick for his personal information. "You can bet I'll be watchin' for ya. Outlaws got a way of startin' young an' never git shed o' the habit. Can't make a crooked stick straight, ya know."

"Hey, Wilber, lay off the boy," I warned when I saw tears well up in Dick's eyes.

"Why should I?" snarled the warden. "Hey, I fergot to check yer license. Lemme see it."

"You mean the blue button pinned to my creel? You should have noticed it while you were pouring my stuff on the ground."

"Where'd you git such a smart mouth, fella?"

"Teaching school."

"Well, ya can't be much of a teacher if ya didn't learn yer lad to count to six inches."

"And by the size of you," I muttered under my breath, "you haven't learned to count calories."

"What'd ya say? Huh? Is that yer blue Ford up yonder?"

"Yes, *sir!*" I replied sarcastically.

"Well, I'll be lookin' fer that car, smart mouth, anytime you park along my streams. I'll be keepin' an eye out for ya. You betcha!"

The warden did an about-face. Lugging Dick's fish, he stalked off to his own vehicle. He creaked open the driver's side door and squeezed behind the steering wheel. He barked at his deputy to "git in the car" and then ground the Jeep into gear. He shook his hambone fist at me as they jolted off down the road trailing exhaust smoke.

I glared at the Willies until it rattled out of sight. Afterward, I stooped to gather up my equipment. Dick needed encouragement, too. Wilber's ruthless behavior had crushed the boy, and he crawled in my Ford in stunned silence. We were both too upset to go home, so I drove farther into the Allegheny Highlands to cool off.

After a few minutes, I could see Dick's anger working on his face. Suddenly, he exploded into a tirade of garbled expletives that included "pus gut," "fat jerk," and "lardass." Finally, he cried in frustration, "Gee, Mr. R, and I didn't get to eat my fish!"

Being Dick was in the wrong, there wasn't much I could say to that. I didn't want to start preaching to him, so I stared out the window at the dense woods until we reached another tributary of the Allegheny River. On the other side of a stone bridge, we saw Wilber's Willies parked directly behind a junker truck.

"Looks like the warden's up to his old tricks," I said, pulling off the dirt road. "Let's check it out."

A scared look passed over Dick's face, and he reluctantly followed me down the path to the creek. We sneaked along sticking to the shadows until we saw a grizzled fisherman. He was crouched under a towering hemlock that grew at the head of a long, deep pool. We crept within twenty-five yards of him and could plainly hear him whistling "Camptown Ladies." Wilber was nowhere to be seen, but Dick and I knew he was lurking about somewhere.

It wasn't long before the old fisherman snagged into a nice trout and began playing it on his bamboo fly rod. After he landed the foot-long brownie, he clunked it on the head and tossed it into a cloth sack that sat behind the hemlock. He then fished another live minnow from a dented bucket and threaded it skillfully on his hook.

In the next fifteen minutes the fisherman caught and kept eight more browns and was playing another. He just hauled the last trout up on the beach when Wilber, accompanied by his deputy, stepped out from behind a screen of brush. "Hey, Hawkins," he barked. "Lemme see yer fish!"

The man called Hawkins calmly unhooked the squirming brownie and put his thumb in its mouth. With a flick of his wrist, he broke the fish's neck and then took out his thin-bladed filet knife. He inserted the blade into the trout's bung hole and slit it to the gills. After pulling out its insides, he held up the glistening fish.

"See?" he chortled.

Dick began laughing like crazy, and I put a finger to my mouth to silence him. Just then, Wilber barked, "Lemme see yer other fish!"

Hawkins limped around the hemlock and opened his gunny sack. He dropped the trout inside and then wiped his hands on his grease-stained overalls.

"They're in there, Wilber."

The warden smiled coyly, and a crater-like dimple stood out on his chin. "What's the limit fer trout, Hawkins?" he asked, barely containing his joy.

"You know as well as me that it's eight."

"Well, I just seen you land ten. Who knows how many others ya snagged before I come along."

"Sure you ain't been hittin' the sauce again, Wilber?"

"I've been tryin' to catch you fer a long time, Hawkins. You're the biggest poacher in my district. Now, I got all the evidence I need right in that burlap bag. I sure must be livin' right! You're the second outlaw I pinched today."

Wilber gave the old fisherman's gunny sack a kick, and the bag began to writhe and jump. "Looks like ya got a couple of beauties. Too bad I'll have ta confiscate 'em."

Remembering the loss of his own trout, Dick groaned when Wilber picked up the bag. Immediately, a warning buzz issued from inside, and the cloth near the warden's leg bulged out as something lunged at him. He dropped the bag like it had burned his fingers and then wailed, "Git them brownies out o' there, Hawkins!"

The fisherman's lips formed into a wry smile beneath his beard. "If you want 'em bad enough,

Wilber, you'll have ta reach in over *my* warden an' fetch 'em yerself."

The rattler guarding Hawkins' fish buzzed again, and Wilber's face went pale. Although Dick and I tried our darnedest to keep still, we snickered like hell at Wilber's dismay. He was too busy avoiding danger to see us leave our hiding place.

Dick said we should flatten the warden's tires when we got back to road, but I nixed that idea. "We don't want to block in Hawkins' truck," I explained with a wink. "I'll bet he plans to fish another stream before dark."

Fierce When Roused

Roland's trembling became more pronounced as he neared the mouth of an alley that met the street ahead. He cradled his lunch pail like a football in the crook of his arm and prepared to break into a sprint. His steel-toed brogans would slow him down, but he couldn't help that. They were required footwear at the B&S where he worked as a machinist on the graveyard shift.

Nightly, he solved technical problems while creating his designs. This problem, though, had no solution. The cops turned a deaf ear to his complaints, and the neighbors slammed their windows to shut out his pleas for help. He had thought of carrying a pistol, but what if he hit some kid riding his bike or a mother pushing a baby stroller? Running was all there was left to do, and he became quite good at it since spring had unleashed a monster upon him.

Roland had reason to be fearful. He just drew even with the alley when a deep growl thundered from the shadows. He turned to face the menace and saw the black form of an advancing beast. His attacker was half German shepherd and half hellhound. When it growled again, muscles rippled beneath the fur of its stout neck. It bared its fangs, and the reek of horsemeat permeated its rank breath. Its eyes glowed jack-o-lantern yellow as it leaped forward with snapping jaws.

In an instant, Roland was in full flight. His shoes slapped against the brick pavement as he raced ahead with the brute loping along behind him — closing fast. His breathing came in rasps, and he now regretted smoking two packs of cigarettes a day. He coughed up black tar and expectorated in the street while the beast continued to gain ground. He could hear its excited yips when he stumbled and almost fell. Its teeth clacked inches from his straining calves, and he shot ahead with renewed fervor.

Sweat streamed down Roland's neck. The street swam before his dizzy eyes. He could just now see his front porch looming from the fog on the right. He worked his rubbery legs and wheezed and prayed until floorboards clattered beneath his feet. He ripped open the front door and slammed it shut just before the hound could plant its fangs in his buttocks.

Roland heard the brute crash against the closed door and then emit a disappointed whine. The exhausted man slid to the living room floor. He gasped and groaned until his own dog padded across the carpet to lick his face and wag its bushy tail.

"Good boy," panted Roland. "Good old Duke. Good old boy."

As Roland hugged Duke, his ninety-year-old grandma limped from the kitchen. She wore a tattered bathrobe that had once been bright blue. Her white hair was tied up in a bun. Although she was deaf as a post, that didn't diminish the fire burning in her eyes. Frowning grimly, she waved her cane at him and spat, "Run again, did you, boy? Instead of a lunch pail, carry a brick!"

The next night at work, Roland mulled over the strategies he had tried on his nemesis. He had always been good with dogs and was totally baffled as to why he hadn't won this hound over. First, he showed no fear, stood his ground, and quietly talked to it. When he held out his hand to give the brute a sniff, it had tried biting it off. Next, Roland bribed it with hotdogs and then a steak. That had only made it hungrier for his blood! Taking the offensive didn't work, either. He had squirted it with ammonia, pelted it with stones, and growled and snarled back. Every time he was forced to outrun the perverse beast or be turned into hamburger.

After punching the time clock at seven a.m., Roland decided to run home. He had changed into a pair of sneakers and left his heavy work shoes in his locker. He jogged from the plant and had already gotten a good head of steam by the time he reached the dreaded alley. The hound was crouched and waiting and wasted no time in attacking. Its growls seemed more ferocious, too, which unnerved Roland. It kept closing until he broke its stride by hurling his lunch pail in its path. He heard his thermos smash inside, but at least he got home without getting chomped.

"Where's your lunchbox?" asked Granny when Roland came bursting in the door.

"Um. . .dropped it."

"Well, don't drop this," snapped the old woman, handing Roland her cane. "That mutt chased you one time too many! Now, let me show you how to defend yourself."

On the way home the next morning, Roland's step was light, and a whistle issued from his lips. Gripping the cane in his right hand, he slashed and stabbed with it and brandished it like a sword. He practiced his footwork, too, once more clad in steel-toed shoes.

Roland walked boldly into the mouth of the alley. A vicious snarl greeted his intrusion. He crouched low like his granny had instructed and held the cane in front of him. The dog sidled around a garbage can overflowing with beer bottles. It surged ahead, foaming at the mouth. Hackles of fur were raised on its back, and its growls intensified into sharp barks. Roland swung his weapon when the dog rushed him but missed by inches. He fended off its fangs by kicking it in the chops.

Sullenly, the brute circled, waiting for an opening. When it leaped at him again, Roland swung the cane with all his might. He brought it down on the middle of the dog's skull, and the brute slumped senseless to the ground. Granny had hollowed out the business end of the cane and filled it with lead. Roland's family motto was "Fierce when roused."

The Attack

The attack began with the shrill of whistles that sent us doughboys scrambling from our trenches. The first to emerge were killed by German snipers. The rest of us streamed across no-man's land through an eerie fog created by last night's bombardment. We dodged shell holes and ruined dwellings and wormed through strung barbed wire.

The closer we got to the Boche lines, the more intense their fire became. Machine guns raked us, and artillery blew big gaps in our ranks, filling the air with blood and debris. The falling shells did terrible work. Mangled bodies were blown in all directions. The shell holes were plastered with bloody bits of flesh.

With so many corpses to feast upon, no wonder the rats got as huge as coons. At night, they carried off our rations and bags of ammo and grenades. They are building a rodent army that we loathe more than the Huns.

A quarter of our regiment was shot to ribbons by the time we spied the Jerrys dug in along the edge of the woods. Wearing helmets that covered their ears, they looked like miscreant football players huddled in the mud. Their gray uniforms were the color of that muck, making them more difficult targets.

Firing madly with our .45 Colt pistols, we officers yelled until we were hoarse. Our soldiers fixed bayonets and followed us into the enemy trenches. We shot and stabbed and took no prisoners. The only good Boche is a dead one.

After machine gunning ten of my command, one coward laid down his empty weapon, raised his hands, and called "Kamerad!" My reply was a bullet in his brain. I laughed when he died.

As we entered the woods, two Hun planes swooped from the sky with guns blazing. They were fighters with Maltese crosses emblazoned on their wings. They barked trees over our heads but did no damage to us. Before they could make a second run, a flight of Spads drove the swine off.

We spread out, crossed a stream, and sneaked up a wooded hill. We immediately encountered a machine gun nest that raked the oaks and punched a line of bullets through the chests of three privates. Hitting the ground, we returned fire with our Colts and Springfields while our scouts crept up on the Huns. Hurling grenades in amongst them, the scouts dispatched the bastards with one big blast!

We had only advanced a short way further when Sarge saw machine gunners coming up on our flank. They were dressed in olive drab and hailed us in English.

"None of our boys should be over there," barked Sarge. "Let 'em have it!"

We wheeled and pumped so many rounds into the intruders that they didn't have time to react. When we inspected their riddled bodies, we found disguised Huns.

"That's what we do to spies and weasels!" growled Sarge, spraying the nearest corpse with tobacco juice.

"What gave them away to you?" I asked.

"Look at their machine guns, sir. They ain't Hotchkisses like our boys use."

When we reached the crest of the hill, we saw a line of entrenchments ahead through the trees. We heard German officers scream commands, and a horde of infantry spilled from their trenches to rush us. They outnumbered our unit at least two to one, but we stopped them with our pinpoint shooting.

While the Huns milled around, we flung the last of our Pineapples into their midst. A pitcher at Dartmouth, I filled the "strike zone" with grenades until the shrieks of the enemy punctuated each explosion. I cheered when they broke and ran.

As dusk fell over the forest, the Jerrys attacked us again. We bunched our machine guns in our center and our BAR's on both flanks. Our automatic weapons staggered them, and our counterattack broke their spirit. With our curses ringing in their ears, they retreated into the gloom.

The night was short and long at the same time. With no blankets to cover us, we shivered in the mud scratching at our cooties. Too wired to sleep, we kept our ears open. There was no way the sneaky Boche would creep up on us!

As soon as it was light, a third offensive issued from the German lines. This time it was led by elite troops with flame throwers. Instead of barbecuing us like they planned, our riflemen turned the fire on them. Shooting the gas tanks strapped to their backs, we cooked the Huns until their flesh sizzled. When their front rank was wrapped in an inferno, the rest turned and fled!

It was then that our artillery dropped in on the party. Shells meant for the enemy rained on us instead. Mountains of earth exploded around us, followed by the shriek of shrapnel. After half our force was maimed or killed, the barrage ended as inexplicably as it began. But what else can be expected in Hell?

When the ground quit shaking, we who survived counted heads and reloaded our weapons. "Our only hope is to play dead," I grunted. "To rise up when they're among us. Shoot them in the faces. Raise such a din they'll think we've gone mad."

In truth, we were already there. Soon, the Hun bastards would feel our full fury!

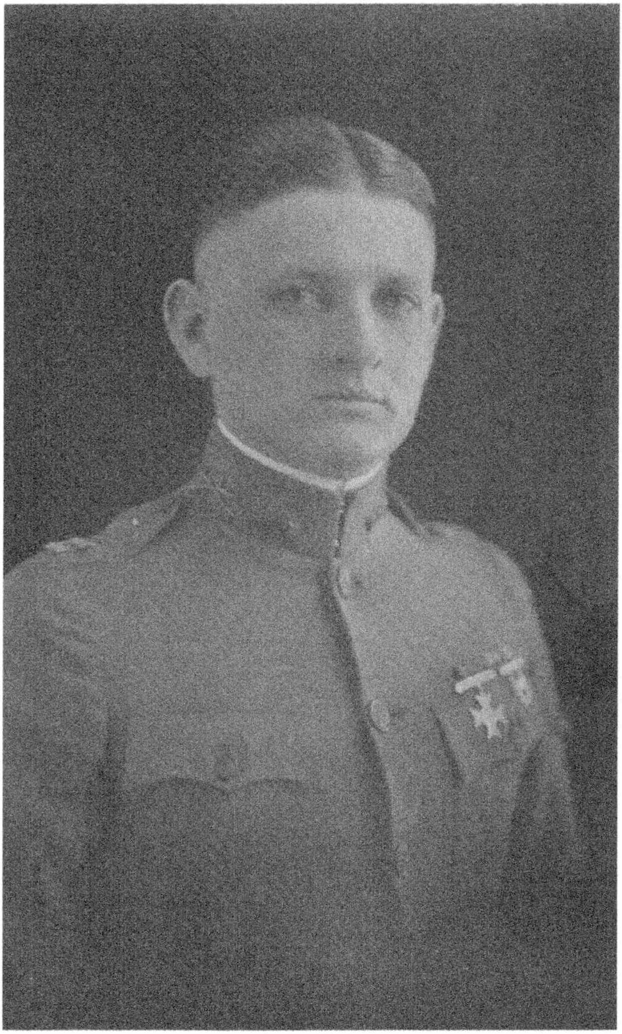

The Ace of Fire

The first flickers of dawn streaked the sky crimson when Mick closed the barrack's door and stepped smartly toward the airdrome of the 85th R.A.F. Squadron. His thin face bore a serious look, and his eyes had a fixed expression. If he hadn't been dressed in leather and sheepskin, he might have been an accountant headed for work instead of a feared flying ace.

The doors of the airdrome were already open, and he saw his S.E. 5 fueled and ready. It was a sleek fighting machine armed with a Vickers gun synchronized to fire through the propeller. He also had a Lewis gun mounted on the top wing just above the cockpit. For an added edge, Mick wanted a cannon installed between his engine blocks like the French used. When none were available, he shot incendiary bullets at the craft he hunted.

If the planes burn, you know they're gone, he thought to himself. *A flamer is always a confirmed victory.*

It wasn't that Mick hated the Huns individually. It was more that his emotions were cauterized by the death he had witnessed. The life expectancy of a fighter pilot was only three weeks on the Western Front. Mick had survived two years. Now, he was doing his job as efficiently as a flight mechanic or a worker in a munitions plant. He, though, was a professional killer, and a cold one at that.

Mick taxied down the bumpy runway and was airborne in a swirl of fog. Half-hidden in the murk, he cruised toward German airspace. Thus concealed, he flew undetected past the Archy antiaircraft gunners and then scanned the skies for enemy two-seaters. Observation planes were his usual target, for they spied on the Allied lines and directed artillery fire wherever the British massed their troops.

It's my job to knock down the Germans' useful planes and save the lives of our infantry, he mused matter-of-factly. *How I do it is my business.*

It wasn't long before a flight of Rumplers emerged from the clouds ahead. Mick climbed his plane well above the clumsy, black-crossed ships and saw there were no accompanying fighters to protect them. Diving out of the sun, he closed quickly on the trailing two-seater and dispatched the rear gunner with a deadly burst from his Vickers. His second burst riddled the gas tank. Immediately, the plane erupted into flames and plummeted toward the ground trailing black smoke.

"Sizzle, sizzle, wonk!" yelped Mick, making a circular gesture with his finger. "One less blighter to snitch on us Brits."

Before the other gunners could draw a bead on him, Mick dove his biplane until the scream of wing wires hummed in his ears. Drawing up beneath the next Rumpler's blind spot, he stitched the belly of the ship under both cockpits with his Lewis gun. He gloated when he saw a spray of blood spew upward from the rear compartment in the fuselage.

Chuckling to himself, Mick recited a droll poem he had heard in last night's mess:

> "Kaiser Bill went up the hill
> To take a look at France.
> Kaiser Bill went down the hill
> With bullets in his pants."

Mick fired again and again. After his third burst, the two-seater's engine sputtered and died. Falling out of formation, the ship glided toward a distant farm field. Disappointed that it hadn't burned, Mick followed the aircraft to the ground.

"Damn incendiary rounds didn't do their job," he muttered. "Next time I'll load my guns with Buckinghams. If they explode hot air balloons, they'll do nasty work on a plane!"

Somehow, the German kept his Rumpler aloft long enough to clear a grove of trees. He landed her by clattering through a series of ruts that spun the ship sideways and choked him with dust. When he finally skidded to a stop, he clambered from his seat, waving his arms jubilantly. It was the last passion he felt before Mick ripped him apart with a hail of bullets.

With his eyes blazing, Mick landed next to the downed aircraft to collect proof of his day's second kill. He was too far behind enemy lines for spotters to see this crippled bird go down, so he cut the squadron identification from its unperforated side. For good measure, he ripped the bloody goggles from the dead pilot's head as a personal souvenir.

The British ace had just returned to his cockpit when the whine of bullets zipped past his helmet. A Hun infantry patrol spewed from the woods and fired frantically at the barbarian who had vanquished their two-seater and murdered its pilot on the ground.

Mick spun his plane in a tight circle until his Vickers came to bear on the charging troops. After annihilating their ranks, he gunned his engine and rumbled off down the field. With his wheels clipping the top branches of the tree line, he cleared it by inches only to find a flight of triplanes circling him like red-feathered buzzards.

It was Mick's rule to never fight scouts unless he had the advantage of surprise. Now, it was his turn to be ambushed, and he fled before the maneuvering pursuit ships that riddled his plane with accurate blasts of gunfire. Soon, everything dissolved in a blur of action. He tried evasive dives and Immelmann turns but was unable to escape the fighters that buzzed around him. His fuselage was pierced from front to back, but miraculously his gas tank had survived. There were holes punched through his leather jacket, too, and a bullet had seared a crimson gash across his forehead. In desperation, he tried a loop to get behind his closest pursuer. As he performed the maneuver, he felt faint and lapsed into unconsciousness.

When Mick righted his ship, the Huns were nowhere in sight. He had entered a thick cloud that bore rain and thunder. The rain made him shiver while the thunder rattled his brain. His gas gauge was nearly on empty, but the engine hummed along as normal as ever. If his compass was correct, he'd soon return to his own lines.

Mick emerged from the thunderhead to find the Fokkers waiting for him. Before he could roll away, his plane was strafed by the flight leader's Spandau machine guns. When flames licked into his cockpit, the ace drew a pistol and held it to his head.

In the end, Mick couldn't pull the trigger. Instead, he went into a deep dive to extinguish the fire. Smoke choked him and obscured his vision.

Just above a forest he pulled up with flames still burning around him.

There was only one thing left to do. Jump! When he climbed onto the bottom wing of his S.E. 5, he saw a river. Closing his eyes, he stepped into space and hurtled toward the water below. He thought of his mother and the green Irish countryside. The war was now over for him. Along with his pyromania.

Father's Gift

Jack peered at the short .22 rifle clutched resolutely in his liver-spotted hands. His aged eyes scrutinized the barrel until he read the Remington 514 model number inscribed there. The gun was a single shot bolt-action that his father had customized for him when he was barely old enough to hold it. Dad shortened the stock so it fit him perfectly and painted the front sight red to make it more visible. Then, he said in a serious, no-nonsense tone, "Before I show you how this gun works, you must promise that you'll never point it at anything you don't intend to kill. This is not a toy, Junior. It's a deadly weapon even in the hands of a five-year-old like you."

Jack's eyes grew misty as he remembered the happy hours of practice that followed his father's safety instructions. First, he fired at paper targets in the backyard while Dad encouraged him to squeeze the trigger and follow through. After shooting a box of ammunition, he was finally able to group his bullets low and left of the bull's-eye. This led to a lesson in adjusting the gun's open sights for height and windage. When he hit the black for the first time, his dad yelled, "That's it, Son! A few more clicks to the right, and there won't be a varmint safe within fifty miles!"

After the gun was sighted in, Jack's dad took him to a garbage dump in the woods. There's where the real fun began, and the old man grinned as he again gunned down exploding, water-filled bottles in the dim glades of his memory. This led him to recall hunting expeditions to nearby ponds where he and his dad stalked greenies and bullfrogs that croaked and grumped in the reeds. By then, they called the short, handy .22 "the potshoter," for it was the perfect weapon for pointing and firing at half-submerged frogs' heads at close range. The sizzle of frogs' legs in the iron skillet testified to its accuracy after every hunt.

"But this gun is accurate at long range, too," mumbled Jack, drawing the rifle to his shoulder. Then, he remembered how his dad had demonstrated its lethal reach one hot summer day while road hunting. They had been driving down a bumpy, dirt track through endless farm fields when the family Fairlane lurched suddenly to a stop. Lifting a hand from the steering wheel, Dad pointed through the windshield at a distant woodchuck whose fur glistened reddish brown in the noonday sun. The critter had its head and shoulders stuck out of a hole a hundred yards off.

Dad creaked open the car door, slipped into the roadside ditch, and assumed a rock-steady prone position. When Jack stole to his side and handed him the potshoter, he trained the sights on the center of his quarry's head. The gun cracked, and immediately the chuck ducked down. Jack wanted to see if it was dead, but his father was busy reloading. "No, I mighta missed," he said. "Let's wait and see."

Dad's hunch proved true when a few minutes later a blunt head again popped from the distant burrow. Aiming more carefully than before, he fired a second time and heard a "thwack" follow the report of his rifle. Leaping to his feet, he strode across the parched fields with Jack on his heels. He raised clouds of dust with each giant step he took. When he found *two* dead groundhogs in the hole, Dad bellowed, "Well, I'll be dipped! This sure is a sweet-shootin' piece. I'd rate her right up there with the Springfield I carried in the war, Sonny Boy."

Jack recalled nodding in wide-eyed admiration at his father's marksmanship. Then, it was his turn to shoot, and he made three clean kills in the next farmer's lot. All the shots had been through the heart and were from fifty yards or more.

This farmer paid Jack a dollar each for the woodchuck carcasses. "Thanks fer riddin' me o' them varmints," he said. "One of m' horses busted a leg in their gol-dang holes, an' I had to put her down. You fellas are welcome to hunt here anytime!"

From that point on, all Jack wanted to do was shoot. To feed his passion, he joined the high school rifle team. He and his teammates practiced in the school basement and kept their target rifles in their lockers before away meets. When they won the National Championship, there was a parade for them down Main Street and everything. Yes, they were real heroes in the 1970's. They got letter jackets the same as the football jocks and track guys.

After graduating, Jack remembered working a series of lousy jobs in order to buy his own deer rifle. The hunting he did with that .06 kept him in good physical shape well into his seventies. If he wasn't in shape, he wouldn't have been ready for today...

The sound of nearby gunfire returned Jack to reality. Staring down his backstairs, he saw a storm trooper sprawled dead at the bottom with a neat bullet hole in his windpipe. He had shot the rascal in the only vulnerable place in his olive drab body armor of Russian design. His helmet and face shield made him look vaguely frog-like, and Jack laughed bitterly and spat, "The potshoter can still drill greenies, even mutant ones! See how many of my guns you collect now!"

Jack gave the .22 a loving pat. His father had traveled halfway around the world to fight the Nazis, so he could hold this gun in his hands. No one was going to steal his father's gift. Not frog-headed storm troopers. Or the evil president who sent them!

Jack never felt the bullet that struck him in the eye. He fired instinctively as he fell, mortally wounding his assailant. This was a corporal who had learned shooting as a trade in Moscow. While the rest of the Russian squad hustled around the corner, Jack tumbled dead down the stairs.

The mercenaries had to hack off the old man's wrists to wrest away his potshoter. His death grip spooked them as they deployed down the smoky street to secure the weapons from the next household. Bullets whined over their helmets as they stole along. Shotguns, muzzleloaders, and hunting rifles created a fearful din. Muttering guttural curses, they wished they had demanded more rubles before attempting this deadly op. Minute Men were now more than legends from an American history text.

Ibin

Ibin exchanged the hell of home for that of no-man's land. Night after night he shivered in the mud as the swoosh of incoming missiles confused like parental putdowns. Explosions pummeled like father's fists as the blue swirl of searchlights probed and probed for him.

An oversized helmet cut Ibin's ears as he turned out for rollcall. His cheeks were a minefield of peach fuzz and grime. Captain smelled his sweat three ranks away.

Ibin enlisted when boys were meat for machine. Steel sergeants booted him through basic until bruises were his badge. Only incendiary detonations lit those cinder eyes.

He lived until spider tanks careened across shell-pocked plains. There was no time to seek escape, and screams provided poor defense against two tons of doom. Death was Ibin's passport as well as his fortune.

Bibliography

"150th Pennsylvania Volunteers Regimental History," <http://www.geocities.com/Pabucktails/150thHistory.html> (21 June 2015).

"1920s Cars," <https://www.google.com/search?q=1920s+cars&tbm=isch&tbo=u&so> (13 July 2015).

"1920's Fashion for Men: A Complete Suit Guide,"<http://www.vintagedancer.com/1920s/1920s-fashion-men/> (12 July 2015).

"American Bullfrog," <http://www.aqua.org/explore/animals/American-bullfrog?gclid=CNKd...> (19 June 2015).

"American Bullfrog," <en.wikipedia.org/wiki/American_bullfrog> (19 June 2015).

Arthur, Max. *The Faces of World War I*. London: Cassell Illustrated, 2007.

"Assassination of Abraham Lincoln," <http://en.wikipedia.org/wiki/Assassination_of_Abraham_Lincoln> (21 June 2015).

Chamberlin, Thomas. *History of the One Hundred And Fiftieth Regiment, Pennsylvania Volunteers. Second Regiment, Bucktail Brigade.* Philadelphia: J. B. Lippincott Company, 1895.

Costik, Sally Ryan. *Bootleggers Bullets and Blood: Bradford Gangsters of the Roaring Twenties.* Bradford: 2011.

"Coyote," <en.wikipedia.org/wiki/Coyote> (4 July 2015).

Hoff, Thomas A. *U.S. Doughboy: 1916-1919.* Oxford: Osprey Publishing, 2005.

Lingle, Melvin G. *Legends of Clearfield County.* State College, PA: Jostens Commercial Publications, 2004.

Finnessy, John J. *The History of the Fifty-Ninth Infantry Regiment.* Unpublished Manuscript.

Hemingway, Ernest. *In Our Time.* New York: Charles Scribner's Sons, 1970.

"Potpourri: Slang of the 1920's," <http://local.aaca.org/bntc/slang/slang.htm> (9 July 2015).

"President Lincoln Assassinated Friday Night!" *The Olean Advertiser*, April 20, 1865, p.2.

"'Round the Square," *The Bradford Era*, April, 14, 2015, p. 1.

Schroeder, Patrick A. *Pennsylvania Bucktails: A Photographic Album of the 42nd, 149th, & 150th Pennsylvania Regiments*. Daleville, VA: Schroeder Publications, 2001.

Sculley, Francis X. *Lost Treasures of Northern Pennsylvania*. Valley Dollar Saver, 1974.

"Security," <www.mrlincolnswhitehouse.org> (21 June 2015).

Sky Fighters of World War I. Ed. Larry Eisinger. Greenwich, Connecticut: Fawcett Publications, Inc., 1961.

The Holy Bible. Cleveland, OH: The World Publishing Company, 1959.

The Lost Brigade. Michael Weisbarth, Executive Producer. New York: A&E, 2001.

Author's Profile

William P. Robertson was born in 1950 in Bradford, Pennsylvania. He graduated from Mansfield University in 1972 with a B.S. in English. He has since worked in factories, taught high school English, and run a successful house painting business. In his spare time, Bill enjoys trout fishing, photography, and rock & roll music.

Robertson began freelancing short stories, poetry, and articles in 1978, and his work has now appeared in over 500 magazines worldwide. He has also published eleven poetry books, thirteen novels, five collections of macabre tales, and an autobiography titled *Stories from the Olden Days*. For more information about Bill's writing, visit http://www.bucktailsandbroomsticks.com.

Also From Infinity Publishing

Stories From the Olden Days
A Humorous Look at Growing Up in the 1950's & '60's

William P. Robertson

B illy Robertson was born in 1950 and grew up in a rural suburb of Bradford, Pennsylvania. Told from the boy's point of view, *Stories from the Olden Days* traces Billy's rollercoaster ride through childhood. The mainly humorous episodes relate his troubles at school, at play, and even at church. Brutal teachers, treacherous classmates, and his quirky family all come under scrutiny as the plot unfolds. He also reveals the incidents and people that influenced him to become a writer. Come join in the games, jokes, and fun from an era uninfected by political correctness.

Stories from the Olden Days is available from Infinity Publishing at www.buybooksontheweb.com or by phoning (887) BUYBOOK. To order a postpaid autographed copy, send $15.50 to Bill Robertson at P.O. Box 293, Duke Center, PA 16729. Make checks payable to Bill Robertson. *Stories* is also available on the web in Kindle, iPad, and Nook e-book formats.

ALSO FROM INFINITY PUBLISHING

The Alleghenies series by William P. Robertson and David Rimer tells the story of Lightnin' Jack Hawkins and his longhunter pals, who hunted and trapped in the primordial forests of colonial Pennsylvania during the 1750's. Dangers lurked everywhere there in the form of ferocious beasts, scalp-stealing savages, and white water rivers of immense fury. The first book details the mountain men's involvement in the Battle of Fort Necessity and the Battle of Braddock's Defeat as the French and Indian War set the frontier ablaze. *Attack in the Alleghenies* continues the adventure when the

Delaware warriors of Shingas and Captain Jacobs go on the warpath to wreak havoc on the English settlers.

The books are available in paperback from Infinity Publishing at www.buybooksontheweb.com or by phoning (887) BUYBOOK. To order a postpaid autographed copy, send $18 for each book to Bill Robertson at P.O. Box 293, Duke Center, PA 16729. Make checks payable to Bill Robertson. The Alleghenies series is also available online in Kindle, iPad, and Nook e-book formats.

The Bucktail Novel Series

William P. Robertson collaborated with David Rimer on a seven-novel series about the original Bucktail Regiment—the 42nd Pennsylvania Volunteers. Acting as skirmishers for the Union, these sharpshooters were the equivalent of today's Army Rangers. The series traces the adventures of Bucky Culp and Jimmy Jewett, two frontier lads who stand the test of fire at Dranesville, Antietam, Gettysburg, and the Wilderness. Also detailed are the brutal marches, lousy rations, inept generals, and fearful diseases that made survival a true test of courage for these young riflemen. The first four novels were published by White Mane while Infinity Publishing produced the last three. For more information, visit http://www.bucktailsandbroomsticks.com.

William P. Robertson

CPSIA information can be obtained
at www.ICGtesting.com
Printed in the USA
BVOW09s0433200617
487341BV00003B/8/P